The End of the Line

by

Andrew Hawthorne

DI Redding Series - Book 4

Edited by Christopher Watt

Copyright: Andrew Hawthorne (2023). All rights reserved.

Cover image created by Jack Hawthorn using CRAIYON.

Prologue

"A serial killer is conventionally defined as a person who murders three or more people in a period over a month, with "cooling down" time between murders. For a serial killer, the murders must be separate events, which are most often driven by a psychological thrill or pleasure. Serial killers often lack empathy and guilt, and most often become egocentric individuals; these characteristics classify certain serial killers as psychopaths. Serial killers often employ a "mask of sanity" to hide their true psychopathic tendencies and appear normal, even charming."

crime.museum.org

Chapter 1

15 November 2019

Grace Anderson was sitting on the train, heading home from Glasgow, feeling incredibly pleased with herself. She had just been promoted at work and had decided to celebrate her good news with some of her closest work colleagues. After having dined in her favourite restaurant, they finished the night off with a few cocktails in a nearby bar. As a result, Grace was feeling a little bit tipsy by the time she caught the train. Her husband, Barry, was just as delighted as she was when she told him her good news earlier that day – they needed the extra money to help pay off their considerable debts. Barry and Grace were now in their late forties and were starting to think seriously about their long-term financial future - they only had the one child – Mark, who was studying at Strathclyde University and, hopefully, would find a decent job. *Life was good.*

Grace glanced at her reflection in the train window, admiring how well she looked for her age. Her long blonde hair was still in good condition, despite the regular bleaching, and her pale skin was still smooth, with only a few wrinkles formed around the sides of her bright blue eyes. She noticed that she had already caught the attention of some of the males sitting within sight of her in the carriage; their eyes immediately dropped as she looked around briefly making eye contact with them, letting them know that she was aware of their inappropriate stares. She was an attractive woman but staring was just rude, regardless of the reason. Her thought pattern was interrupted by the automated announcement triggered by the train pulling into Coatbridge Sunnyside station. *Nearly home*, she thought. Grace fastened her long coat and held her bag in her lap, ready to get off at the next stop.

Coatdyke was a small residential area located between the neighbouring towns of Coatbridge and Airdrie and had improved significantly in recent years due to the wealth created by the large influx of workers based at the Monklands General Hospital. Grace and Barry had moved there just after the hospital had opened; it was convenient for

Barry, who worked there as a Charge Nurse and often had to work the night shift.

As the train pulled into the long six-carriage platform at Coatdyke, Grace stood up and stopped at the door, waiting for the exit light to signal that it could be opened. She was followed by a middle-aged man wearing a long dark blue overcoat, smart black trousers and black training shoes which looked a wee bit out of place. Grace quickly dismissed his poor dress sense and paid no further attention to him.

She stepped off the train tentatively, thus ensuring that she did not slip on the damp surface. She had chosen to wear her new black patent leather shoes instead of her more boring flat-soled work shoes and although they were not that practical for walking any sort of distance due to the one-inch heel, Grace had wanted to look her best for the interview, so the decision had been an easy one, although her feet were beginning to hurt a little now.

With both feet firmly on the concrete platform, Grace quickly made her way down the exit ramp onto Quarry Street and headed towards Lavelle Drive. Her home was only a short distance away on Eglington Street, on the other side of Dumbeth Park. She paused for a moment when she reached Lavelle Drive and then decided to take the shortcut through the park. Barry would be raging but what he didn't know couldn't hurt him.

Grace entered the park, passing the large rusting metal gates and made her way along the path which ran parallel to the railway line. Her long coat, which she had fastened to the bottom to keep her legs warm, restricted how far she could move thus forcing her to walk awkwardly in short scissor-like steps. It didn't take long for her to tire of this awkwardness and so she stopped to unfasten the bottom button of her coat. That's when she heard the footsteps.

She turned to see who was following her and saw it was the man in the long blue overcoat, and although he looked harmless, she decided not to take any chances and started walking as quickly as she could, her heart beginning to race. However, she soon realised that he had increased his speed and was now closing in on her. She panicked and started running as fast as she could in her new shoes. He chased after her and soon caught up; his superior speed and sensible footwear made the task far too easy. Grace could hear him get closer and closer and began to scream out for help but it was too little too late. She turned her head back to see where he was and tripped herself up, falling to the ground, landing hard on her hands. She turned and looked up at him, her eyes full of tears but most of all - fear. Standing over her, he removed his weapon of choice from his coat pocket. The last thing Grace saw was the hammer swing down from above before it smashed into her fragile skull.

The killer looked around to make sure no one had witnessed his first act. Satisfied, he dragged her body behind some large rhododendron bushes, which lined the path. He then raised the hammer and smashed it into her head, repeatedly until all his anger had dissipated and he felt at peace with the world. The release had been everything he had hoped for – but this was only the beginning. There would be more.

Chapter 2

Present Day

Petrie's solicitor, Gordon Wallace, was waiting patiently for his client to be escorted to an interview room, deep in the heart of Barlinnie Prison. Petrie was being held in custody pending trial for the murder of three men: Kevin McGrath, Mick Conroy, and Pat Malloy, all of whom were involved with the sale of cocaine in the Dumbarton area. Detective Inspector Claire Redding and Billy Taylor had witnessed the murders and both had been lucky to avoid the same fate as the deceased.

Petrie was led into the interview room by two prison officers, who then sat him down on the white plastic chair which was positioned directly opposite Wallace.

"You can remove the handcuffs, thank you," Wallace instructed.

The senior of the two officers approached Petrie and removed the cuffs. "There's an alarm button underneath your side of the table. Any trouble and we can be in here in seconds."

"Thank you, officer, but I'm sure that won't be necessary," responded Wallace. He waited for the two men to leave the room, took a folder from his case, and placed it on the white plastic table. Although there were two cameras in the room, which were being monitored in the adjoining room, there were no microphones allowed to ensure client confidentiality.

"So, what's happening?" asked Petrie.

"Well, it's not looking good," said Wallace nervously. "Both DI Redding and Billy Taylor have submitted written statements - I have copies here for you to see. I suggest we go over them carefully - to see if there is anything we can challenge when we get to court, but I have to say both their statements appear to support each other, so they'll be hard to break down." Wallace paused, waiting for a reaction from his client.

Surprisingly, Petrie did not look overly concerned. "I don't think we will need to worry about Billy Taylor for much longer."

Wallace looked up from the folder. "Oh? And why is that?"

"Let's just say a wee birdie told me that he is thinking about withdrawing his statement," said Petrie, grinning.

"Really? Well, that would change things but they still have the statement from DI Redding, so let's go over that, shall we?"

Petrie nodded in response. The two men sat there for over an hour, going over every word of the statement in detail; trying to find something they could use to weaken the police case. Eventually, confident that there was no further work to be done, Wallace packed his case and stood up. Petrie stood up and offered his hand to Wallace who reluctantly shook it. He felt the small piece of paper which Petrie had placed in the palm of his hand and immediately understood that Petrie wanted him to take it without raising any suspicions. He quickly withdrew his hand and, as naturally as he could, put the note casually in his trouser pocket and walked to the door. He knocked twice on the door and heard the lock turning. "We're finished for today," he said to the prison officer, who was standing guard outside the door. The other officer, who had been observing the video from the cameras, came out of the next door along the narrow corridor and joined his colleague. He entered the room and instructed Petrie to put out his hands so that he could cuff him in preparation for the long walk back to his holding cell.

"Dan, if you escort Mr Wallace to the exit, I'll take the prisoner back to his cell," instructed the senior of two men.

Dan nodded. "Follow me, Mr Wallace," he said and marched off down the corridor. After making their way through numerous gates and barriers, Wallace found himself at the public entrance to HMP Barlinnie and walked towards the car park. He got into the car and immediately read the message on the piece of paper that Petrie had passed to him. The message was brief but Wallace knew exactly what it meant. It read:

Danny McCafferty, Dog and Bone - £100k – DI Redding accident.

"Shit!" Wallace said aloud. His stomach churned as he realised the potential repercussions that may follow if he passed on the note. McCafferty, was Manager of Petrie's pub - the Dog and Bone, and clearly Wallace was expected to pass on the message on which would make him a party to the murder of a police officer! *God, could this get any worse?* However, Wallace also knew what would happen to him if he refused to pass on the instruction. That thought was enough to churn his stomach again and this time he couldn't control the urge to throw up. He pushed open the door of his BMW and duly emptied the contents of his breakfast onto the tarmac.

Chapter 3

Detective Inspector Claire Redding was sitting at her desk in 'L' Division HQ, Dumbarton, reviewing a report on a recent break-in at a licensed store in Clydebank. The incident had been recorded on CCTV cameras inside the premises, but the two offenders had been clever enough to disguise their faces with Halloween masks – one was Frankenstein's monster and the other, Count Dracula. They had broken in via the backdoor which had set off the security alarm but by the time the owner had been alerted by the alarm company, the two thieves were long gone with their stash of alcohol and cigarettes. Claire noticed that one of the men was wearing a hoodie with a large print of an eagle on the back and decided that the distinctive image was their only real chance of getting an identification. The SOCO had found some fingerprints at the scene but they would need to be matched on the national database to be of any immediate value. She would run a check on the fingerprints and get copies of the eagle image on the hoodie together, along with a general description of the two men – height and build - circulated to all local police officers operating in the Clydebank area. Satisfied that she had covered everything for the time being, Claire went over to the office kettle to make herself a cup of tea.

"Do you want anything, Brian?" she asked DS O'Neill, who was sitting opposite her in the CID room. Her other colleagues were absent; DC Jim Armstrong was on leave and DC Paul Black was recovering from an almost fatal attack by one of Petrie's henchmen. Claire had also been injured when taking down Petrie and his gang but had made a quick recovery; the bruising to her face had all but disappeared although her nose now had a slight bump on the bridge, where it had been broken by a fierce backhanded slap by Petrie. She had been promised plastic surgery when she had first received treatment but since then had decided not to bother, as much to her surprise, she was told she was pregnant.

"Aye, go on then, a cup of tea would be great. Thanks, boss."

Just as she was about to put the kettle on, her mobile phone rang. She recognised the number - it was Billy Taylor.

"Hello, Billy. How are you?" she asked. Brian looked up and indicated to Claire that he would make the tea since she was now on the phone.

"Hello," he said nervously. Claire could tell something was wrong.

"What's the matter, Billy? Is everything okay?"

"I'm sorry… but I've decided to withdraw my statement."

"What? Why Billy? Has something happened? Has someone threatened you?"

"No… no it's not that. It's just … well … I've been thinking and I don't want to put Maureen in any danger. We've been through enough and well… you don't need my statement to convict Petrie, do you? You were there and saw everything."

Claire could sense that Billy was not telling her the complete truth - someone must have gotten to him. "Billy, if you've received a threat, we can protect you. We talked about this a few weeks ago… remember? I can get you and Maureen on a witness protection programme until the trial is over and…"

"I'm sorry, but I don't want to go through witness protection. I just want to withdraw my statement. I'm sorry but I've made up my mind." The line went dead.

Brian approached Claire holding two cups of tea and offered the cup in his right-hand – the one without sugar. "I guess Billy's not prepared to testify then," he said.

"Yeah, someone has gotten to him. He sounded really scared."

"What about you? Have you been threatened yet?"

"No chance. Petrie wouldn't be that stupid. Well, it looks like it's just me versus Petrie in court - I'd better let the Fiscal's Office know about Billy."

Brian nodded and took a large slurp of his tea. "Shouldn't make much difference though, eh? A police officer's word against that of a well-known villain. The jury would need to be mad to let him off the hook."

"Yes, that or scared to death!" said Claire.

"You don't think Petrie would try to intimidate the jury!" Brian exclaimed.

"I wouldn't rule out anything when it comes to that man."

Chapter 4

Wallace had taken his time to plan what would happen next. He couldn't be directly involved in passing on the instruction to have Redding killed so he used his criminal contacts to find someone who would do his dirty work for him – for a small fee, of course. He typed out Petrie's note onto plain white paper and put it in a plain white envelope. If the police ever got their hands on Petrie's hand-written note, they would know that it must have been passed on by Wallace as he was Petrie's only visitor in Barlinnie. So, typing it onto blank paper made absolute sense as it could not be traced. After careful consideration, Wallace decided to ask Hugh Docherty to deliver the note. Docherty had served time in prison for a robbery which he and his friends had committed a few years back. He had been unlucky as he was the only member of the gang to be caught by the police but, much to Wallace's surprise, Docherty steadfastly refused to grass up any of his friends to reduce his sentence. This was the one quality that Wallace had been looking for but just to be sure he made it clear to Docherty that they were both working for Petrie and therefore there would be consequences if he messed up.

Docherty stood nervously outside the pub. He put on his facemask and entered the front door of the Dog and Bone just after noon. He looked around and could see that the pub was empty. *Perfect.* He headed straight for the bar and asked for Danny McCafferty. The barman didn't ask any questions and immediately went through a door at the back of the bar area and shouted for Danny to come out.

Danny McCafferty had worked for Petrie for many years and had been trusted by Petrie to run the Dog and Bone since it had re-opened. He entered the bar area and spoke briefly to the barman who then pointed over to where Docherty was standing waiting. He nodded to the barman and approached Docherty who took out the plain white envelope.

"Are you Danny McCafferty?"

"Aye, how can I help you?"

"I've a message for you from Mr Petrie." He handed over the envelope.

McCafferty opened the sealed envelope, read the note, and immediately understood the message. "Do you know what this says?" asked McCafferty, holding up the folded notepaper.

"No, I was handed the sealed envelope and told to tell you that it came from Petrie. That's all I know."

"Good. Well, you can tell whoever passed this message on that I will do as instructed. Got it?"

Docherty nodded. "Got it." He turned and left the pub, happy that he had completed his task. That was the easiest five hundred pounds he had ever made.

Chapter 5

Claire and her husband Peter MacDonald sat together on their living room sofa watching the ITV News at Ten. Sally, Peter's spoiled wee Cocker Spaniel, was sitting at his feet sleeping.

Claire felt quite relaxed and cuddled into Peter; her day had been uneventful, other than her brief conversation with Billy Taylor and subsequent chat with the Assistant Procurator Fiscal. Peter, on the other hand, could not relax. He hadn't told Claire about the threatening phone call he had received a few weeks back – the call which made it clear that if Claire testified against Petrie, then she and everyone she loved would die. He had been in shock when the call had ended and had Claire not announced her pregnancy to him just at that moment then he might have told her all about it, but he didn't, and now he felt that he couldn't.

"Is everything okay, Peter?" Claire asked, sensing something was wrong. "Bad day at work?"

Peter cuddled into her and smiled. "No, I'm fine."

"You don't seem fine. Are you sure nothing is bothering you?"

"I'm fine, honest … how was your day? Catch any criminals?" he said, quickly changing the subject.

"It was okay. Although, I had to have an awkward conversation with the Fiscal's Office. Billy Taylor has decided *not* to testify against Petrie! It'll be okay though, the Fiscal thinks that my testimony will be enough to get a conviction but it would have been easier if Billy backed me up in court."

Peter was becoming increasingly anxious. "Did he say why he won't testify?"

"No, but I reckon someone has threatened him. Petrie's still a powerful man and no doubt has paid somebody to scare Billy off."

"I don't blame him," said Peter.

"Who? Petrie?"

"No, Billy, I don't blame him for backing down. If Petrie is as powerful as you say then he could pay someone to hurt or even kill Billy?"

"Yes, he could, which is why I offered him witness protection but he refused that as well."

"I still don't blame him," said Peter. "And what about you? What if Petrie decides to get rid of you?

Then, there would be no witnesses to testify against him!"

"Don't be daft. I'm a police officer. He's hardly going to take that risk, is he?"

Peter didn't respond. He was now even more anxious than before. The joy and excitement of their recent marriage, the news of Claire's pregnancy – all these things should have filled him with happiness, but instead all he felt was dread. He jumped with fright as the house phone rang. Claire was the first to respond and ran into the hall to take the call. It was DS O'Neill.

"Sorry Claire, but the DCI has called us all in. A body has been found in Craigendoran, close to the station. The DCI wants you to meet her out there pronto. I've to stay here to set up an incident room. Oh, and Claire, I should warn you, it's a bad one. Really bad!"

Chapter 6

When Claire arrived at the scene of the crime, the SOCO had already set up a small incident tent around the area where the body was found. The whole of Middleton Lane had been cordoned off with blue police tape; only emergency services staff and their vehicles were allowed anywhere near the scene.

Claire spotted DCI Mitchell standing outside the tent and made her way towards her, occasionally showing her ID to those police officers guarding the perimeter.

"Ah, DI Redding, you finally made it," said the DCI.

Claire ignored the little dig. "Yes, Ma'am. So, what do we have?"

"Have a look for yourself but you'll need to put on full protective clothing first and be careful. There's a lot of blood on the ground in there."

Claire found the SOC vehicle and quickly put on the standard white suit, shoe covers, facemask and goggles. Brian had warned her it was a bad one so she steeled herself before entering the tent. One of the SOCOs was busy taking photographs of the body but stopped and stood back as she entered. She looked down and almost fainted at the sight of what lay in front of her. The dead woman's head and face had been smashed to pieces. Claire took a few breaths and steadied herself before taking a closer look. She could see that the SOCO had marked various parts of the skull and brain tissue which lay splattered around the head area in a pool of blood. Her stomach churned and she quickly left the tent and threw up on the side of the road.

"Still got a weak stomach then," said the DCI as she approached the young detective who was bent over trying to control her stomach spasms. "Don't worry, you'll get used to it… eventually."

"I don't think I'll ever get used to seeing things like that!" responded Claire standing upright to face her DCI. "I thought I was finished with the vomiting for a while now that the morning sickness has settled down but nothing could have prepared me for what's inside that tent."

"Yes, it's a gruesome one but the good news is that we've got the murder weapon and probably have the killer as well," said Mitchell cheerfully.

"You're kidding!" said Claire, wiping her mouth against the sleeve of her overalls.

"We'll need to gather all the forensics first, of course, and hopefully get a confession as the evidence is overwhelming, but we have the deceased's partner, Robert Baird, in custody. It was Baird who called it in and when our boys arrived at the scene; he was found here, sitting beside his partner's body, covered in blood. He's on his way back at the station now. The SOC Team has taken his blood-covered clothing and the murder weapon – a hammer, with a full set of fingerprints."

"What's the victim's name?"

"Sheila Maxwell, age 47. She lived with Baird in Craigendoran Avenue, which is just at the end of the lane."

"Why would he kill her out here and not at home where he could clean up the mess and hide the evidence?" asked Claire.

"It's possible that they had a fight, she left and he chased after her with the hammer. Who knows how a psychopath thinks?"

"Who knows indeed," said Claire struggling to understand how any sane person could commit such a crime. "Okay, so what do you need me to do?"

"I'm going to stay here until the SOC Team has finished their work. I'll also need to deal with the press - they'll be wanting a statement at some point tonight and the Super has instructed our media team to advise me on what to say - bloody cheek! Anyway, I want you and DS O'Neill to interview Baird. Go gently. So far, he's not said anything. See if you can get him to confess so that we can get this case done and dusted."

"Right then, I'd better get going, Ma'am," said Claire, delighted that she had been given the responsibility of interviewing the main suspect in such a high profile case. She stripped off her protective outfit and handed it back to the SOC Team for safe disposal and then made her way back to her car. She called Brian, updated him on what was happening and asked him to prepare interview room 1.

Chapter 7

It took Claire approximately twenty minutes to get back to the Police HQ in Dumbarton. Brian had finished setting up the incident room and had arranged for Mr Baird to be put into room 1, as instructed. Interview room 1 was fully equipped with cameras and audio to record the discussion and also allow others to observe and hear the interview but, on this occasion, no one else was available to observe the interview.

Claire quickly briefed Brian on the DCI's instructions to go gently in the hope of obtaining a voluntary confession and they agreed that Claire should take the lead. They entered the room where Robert Baird was sitting waiting, accompanied by a police officer. Baird was wearing grey jogging bottoms and a matching top, provided by the station. Claire's first observation was that Baird was a broken man; his whole disposition suggested he had suffered a great loss and that he was struggling to cope with it.

"Mr Baird, I am Detective Inspector Claire Redding and this is Detective Sergeant Brian O'Neill. I understand that you were cautioned at the scene of your partner's murder by Detective Chief Inspector Mitchell and would remind you that you are still under caution which means you do not have to say anything but it may harm your defence if you do not mention when questioned something which you might later rely on in court. Anything you do say may be given in evidence. Do you understand?"

"Yes."

"You also have been made aware of your right to have a solicitor present but have declined, is that correct?"

"Yes, but I don't understand, why have I been arrested? I was the one who reported the crime and I was the one who found Sheila, lying there..." He couldn't continue as the pain of his loss suddenly overwhelmed him and tears began to run down his cheeks.

"It's okay, Mr Baird," said Claire sympathetically. "Please, take your time. I understand how upset you must be right now, but you need to consider how bad this looks for you - your clothes were covered in her blood, your finger..." Claire stopped mid-sentence as it was obvious that any mention of the blood or the victim only made matters worse and so she decided to change tact. "Mr Baird. Why don't you tell me what happened tonight?"

Baird gathered himself and sighed before speaking. "I was at home when Sheila texted me to say that she was on the train and had just passed Cardross which meant that she would be home in about ten minutes. That was about 9.35 p.m. We only live a few minutes from the station," he explained.

Claire nodded by way of encouragement. "Right, so what happened next?"

"Well, it was around 9.55 when I suddenly realised that Sheila hadn't come home. I was watching football on the TV and got a bit distracted," he said defensively. "As soon as I realised that she was later than expected, I called her mobile to check what had happened and didn't get a response. I then checked the Trainline App on my phone to see if the train had been delayed, but it hadn't. That's when I started to worry so I put on my jacket and went out to look for Sheila and … and that's when I found her, lying there in the lane, her face and head smashed to …" He broke down and started to weep again.

Claire allowed Baird some time to pull himself together. This was not going to plan. "Mr Baird, you said that Sheila was on the train. Where had she been?"

Baird looked up and wiped his face with the sleeve of his top. "She was visiting her daughter, Irene. She's studying Law at Napier University in Edinburgh – it was her birthday today. Sheila met her in Edinburgh and they both went out for a meal to celebrate."

"I see. I assume you're not Irene's father?" Claire asked.

"No, Sheila was married before she met me and had two girls – Irene and Christine. She's divorced now and ... well ... we never got round to getting married."

"And where does Christine live? With you and Sheila?"

"No, she's in Glasgow - has her own flat. Well, rents a flat with her boyfriend."

"Thank you, Mr Baird. I'm afraid the next set of questions may be a bit upsetting but we have to ask." Claire paused again to allow Baird to compose himself. "You said that you found Sheila lying in the lane? Can you explain how your clothes managed to be covered in blood?"

"Yes, and I'm sorry. I know I shouldn't have touched anything but I was so distraught at the sight of her that I bent down and pulled her towards me." His eyes filled with tears again. He took a deep breath in an attempt to control his emotions and wiped his eyes with the same wet sleeve as before. "I did it without thinking! I know it was a stupid thing to do but, in the moment, well… I didn't care. All I wanted to do was hug her and…" He stopped speaking and started sobbing again, tears filling his bloodshot eyes.

"It's okay Mr Baird. Take your time. I know this is not easy for you," said Claire as softly as she could. "The hammer found at the scene has a set of fingerprints on it. Did you pick it up at any point during your … eh … embrace?"

"I might have. I can't really remember. Wait a minute, yes I did, again another stupid thing to do, I know. When I went to lay Sheila down again, I lost balance and fell forward and put my right hand out to stop me. It was so dark I didn't see the hammer but I felt something hard when my hand pressed against the ground and I instinctively picked it up to see what it was. As soon as I realised that it was a hammer, I put it back in the same spot."

Claire paused for a few moments before continuing. "Okay, Mr Baird, we'll get forensics to confirm that it's your fingerprints on the hammer. So, immediately after hugging Sheila, you called the police, is that correct?"

"Yes."

"And did you call anyone else?"

"No."

"Mr Baird, you mentioned that Sheila was married before you met her and that she was divorced. Was it an amicable separation?"

Baird appeared to relax a little now that the questions had moved away from the crime scene.

"No, it was a bit of a messy affair. Iain wasn't too happy with the outcome. Sheila got the house and custody of the two girls," he explained.

"Iain?"

"Oh sorry, Iain Livingstone. Maxwell was Sheila's maiden name and she reverted to it after the divorce."

"I see, and has there been much contact between Iain and Sheila since the divorce?"

"No, not that I'm aware of … as I said it didn't end well."

"And what about the girls?"

"No, they didn't want to see him after the divorce. I got the impression that they didn't like him; he worked away from home a lot and when he did get home, he didn't have much time for them."

"Do you know where Mr. Livingstone lives now?"

"I've no idea … sorry."

"Okay, thank you, Mr Baird. I'm afraid we'll need to keep you here for a bit longer while we confirm your version of events."

"My version of events?" Do you mean, I'm not free to go home? I've told you everything I know. You can check my phone; you'll see that I'm telling the truth."

"We will Mr Baird, but it will take some time. Are you sure you don't want to see a solicitor?"

Baird put his head in his hands. "I can't believe this is happening – you think I did it, don't you?"

"Mr Baird, right now I don't know what to think. We'll need to verify certain elements of your story and we'll need to wait for the forensic report before making any decision."

"In that case, I do want to see a solicitor," said Baird.

"That's fine. We can arrange for a duty solicitor to attend on your behalf or you can call your own solicitor, if you have one. Oh, and one last thing, we'll need to contact Irene and Christine to let them know about their mother. Can you provide us with details of their addresses and contact numbers?"

"Yes, I suppose so. Oh God, poor Irene, and on her birthday – she'll be absolutely distraught."

~

Claire and Brian left the interview room and headed back along the corridor to the CID Room to confer in private.

"Well Brian, what do you think?"

"I'm not sure, boss. On the one hand, we have him covered in the victim's blood and his fingerprints on the hammer but on the other, we don't have any motive, even if he is some sort of psychopath. Also, why would he kill her in the street and then phone the police? It just doesn't make any sense."

"I agree, so we'll need to confirm everything he said before we do anything. We need to speak to both daughters, especially Irene. I want to get a feel for the relationship between Baird and Sheila Maxwell. Find out if they have been fighting recently. You know what the stats say – most murder victims know their killer."

"And what about Iain Livingstone, her former husband and father to those two poor girls?" asked Brian.

"Yes, we'll need to speak to him too but let's face it, the divorce was settled years ago. I can't see it being him. No, judging by the viciousness of the attack, it had to be either personal or the work of a psychopath … or both."

Brian nodded in agreement.

Claire approached the large office window which faced out onto the A82 and stared out into the darkness. "Well, one thing is for certain - the DCI is not going to be happy when she hears how the interview went. I hope she is careful when briefing the press because this case is far from being done and dusted."

"Cup of tea, boss?" asked Brian.

"Why not, it's going to be a long night."

Chapter 8

DCI Mitchell was far from pleased when Claire briefed her on the outcome of her interview with Baird. She had called the whole team into the incident room for an early morning briefing and had allocated tasks to them all. Brian and Claire had only managed to get a couple of hours of sleep but knew that they were needed and did not gripe when the DCI suggested an unusually early 6 a.m. start. DC Jim Armstrong had been also called in together with a few uniform officers, who would assist with the collation of evidence and manage the telephone calls.

DCI Mitchell decided that she and DS O'Neill would interview Baird; this time in the presence of his solicitor, Robert Strange – a familiar face at 'L' Division HQ. Claire and Jim would interview Iain Livingstone (the ex-husband) as soon as they could track him down. Having spent some time searching the electoral registers for the name Iain Livingstone, Claire and Brian finally tracked him down, living in the Jordanhill area of Glasgow. Thankfully, there were only ten Iain Livingstone's currently registered in Scotland and only five out of the ten lived in the central belt. After a few calls, they identified the right one and arranged for him to be interviewed that morning. Time was of the essence and he agreed to come into Dumbarton early, which suited him as this would allow him to go to work immediately after the interview concluded.

~

Iain Livingstone appeared at the 'L' Division HQ just before 8 a.m. DC Jim Armstrong went down to the reception area to greet him and took him up to interview room 2, where Claire was waiting patiently.

She stood up as the two men entered the room "Hello Mr Livingstone. Please take a seat. I'm DI Redding and this is my colleague, DC Armstrong. Thank you for agreeing to come in at such short notice."

Livingstone smiled politely at DI Redding and sat down without speaking. He was tall, had dark blue eyes and striking blonde hair. If he had been a few years younger Claire might have fancied him but he was clearly in his late forties – far too old for

Claire and age aside, she had Peter and no one else had a look in.

She set her thoughts aside and proceeded with the interview. "Just so we are clear, Mr Livingstone. You are not under arrest and you are not under caution which means you are not obliged to answer any of our questions and can leave at any time. Is that understood?"

"Yes, detective. That's understood. How long will this take? I'll need to be at work for 9 a.m."

"And where is your work, Mr Livingstone?" Claire asked, slightly annoyed by the man's attitude.

"I'm the manager of the Anniesland branch of the TSB," he said pompously.

"A bank manager?"

"Yes, a bank manager," he said sardonically.

Claire noticed his annoyance and decided to get straight to the point. "Okay, Mr Livingstone, when was the last time that you saw Sheila Maxwell alive?"

Livingstone was slightly surprised by the directness of the question. "Oh, now let me think." He took a few moments to gather his thoughts before responding. "It's been such a long time but I think it might have been just after the divorce settlement. I went round to my house to collect a few personal items - I think both Sheila and Baird were there. I took my things and left the house, never to return. So, let's see, that would be about eight years ago - we had been separated for two years before the divorce was finally settled, so yes, about eight years ago."

"And was the divorce an amicable one?" asked Claire.

Livingstone clasped his hands together and then rubbed his face and grinned. "Oh, I see, you've been talking to Baird then. I suppose he told you that it was far from amicable ... and he'd be right. Of course, I wasn't happy with the outcome - I lost my house and I lost my girls. How would you feel if that happened to you? You know there's something wrong with the law of this country when the woman has the affair and gets to keep everything. So, yes, I was angry at the time, but come on detective - that was eight years ago. You don't seriously think I had anything to do with Sheila's murder, do you?"

Claire knew that he had exaggerated the position on the point of law - all joint assets would be divided equally between the two parties, regardless of blame, and clearly, he did blame Sheila, but it was eight years ago. "Thank you for being so frank, Mr Livingstone, I have one more question. Where were you between 9.30 p.m. and 10.00 p.m. last night?"

"I was at the cinema," he said without any hesitation.

"Can anyone confirm that you were there?"

"Well, I went on my own, but I'm sure someone in the cinema could confirm it or you could check their CCTV," he said nonchalantly. He put his hand inside his jacket pocket and removed the wallet. "Ah, yes, here it is." He removed a pink ticket stub from his wallet and handed it to DI Redding to inspect.

Claire looked at the ticket and quickly checked the date and time of the show. She passed it to Jim to double-check. He nodded to Claire. The ticket stub stated that the movie, 'Unhinged' started at 8.00 p.m. Jim, who had already seen the movie knew that it lasted at least two hours long, longer if you included time for the adverts and movie previews, so it would not have been possible for Livingstone to watch the movie and kill Sheila Maxwell.

Claire decided that they had enough information to go on. "Thank you, Mr Livingstone, do you mind if we hold onto the ticket? We'll need to confirm this with the cinema, of course, but this should suffice for now."

"Thank you, Inspector. By all means, hold onto the ticket." He paused before continuing. "May I ask, have the girls been informed of their mother's death?"

Claire was about to respond when there was a knock on the door and DS O'Neill entered the room. "Sorry to interrupt, boss, but the DCI wants to see you right away – there's been a development?"

Chapter 9

Claire closed the interview with Livingstone and headed straight to DCI Mitchell's Office. She knocked on the door and entered the small room where, to her surprise, the DCI was not alone. The two gentlemen, both wearing grey suits, stood up as Claire entered the room. The older of the two men was tall, had grey hair and steely blue eyes. The other man was smaller, had a heavier build and had a significant scar on the side of his face, which Claire guessed was the result of a knife attack.

"DI Redding, this is Detective Superintendent Milligan and Detective Chief Inspector Carter from the Major Incident Team in Glasgow."

Both men took it in turns to acknowledge Claire and sat down again, which meant that Claire was the only person in the room left standing.

DCI Mitchell spoke first. "Claire, there's been a development which has changed the direction of our investigation and consequently MIT will be taking over the case from now on."

"What? What's going on?" asked Claire, more forcibly than she had intended.

The older of the two men, DSup Milligan, was the first to respond to Claire's little outburst. "I'm pleased you feel so… passionate about your work, Inspector, but I'm afraid you do not have any say in the matter. DCI Carter will be taking charge of the investigation and I expect your full cooperation. In fact, DCI Carter's team is a little short on the ground at the moment so we would like you to work with MIT, until we catch the killer."

Claire was taken aback by the offer. She knew that MIT only investigated the most serious crimes and this was a fantastic opportunity for her. "Well, that sounds great, providing DCI Mitchell agrees, but…"

Mitchell interrupted her. "Claire, I have already agreed to assign both you and DS O'Neill to MIT. It appears that your reputation has preceded you and you are both very much in demand." There was more than a hint of jealousy in her tone.

"Thank you, Ma'am, but if I may. Can someone explain why MIT is involved in this case? After all, we have the main suspect in custody and once we get forensics back …"

DSup Milligan interrupted her. "Mr Baird will be released as soon as we leave this office, Inspector. He's not who we are after - we're looking for a serial killer."

"A serial killer? But there's been nothing in the press …"

Milligan interrupted her. "Yes, and we want to keep it that way for as long as we can. The person we are looking for has committed at least two other murders. All have similar MOs: all three victims are blonde middle-aged women, all three had their heads bashed in and in all three cases a hammer was used to inflict the damage and was left at the scene, with all fingerprints wiped clean."

"All except the last murder - we have a full set of fingerprints and the main suspect covered in the victim's blood. How can you be sure that this is the same killer? It could be a coincidence," Claire pointed out.

DCI Carter, who was beginning to lose his patience with the impertinent DI, decided to intervene. "Yes, it could be a coincidence, Inspector, but highly unlikely as we now believe the killer is targeting his victims on the Helensburgh to

Edinburgh train line. All three murder victims were heading home having been on the train. We were not sure if that was just a coincidence but we are now confident that this is the case."

Claire had to agree that there were too many similarities for the murders to be unrelated. "Okay, what if Baird is the serial killer or pretending to be one? The amount of anger and violence used in these attacks… it looks personal to me."

"And how much experience do you have catching serial killers, Inspector?" asked Milligan sarcastically.

"None, sir," she replied in a softer voice.

"None. Exactly!" he snapped. "Well, for your information, DCI Mitchell has already checked Mr Baird's whereabouts at the time of the other two murders and he was able to provide solid alibis for both and this has now been confirmed."

"Oh!" Claire was visibly rattled by that piece of information and suddenly realised that she could be wrong.

Milligan could see the penny had suddenly dropped. "Well, detective? Are you up for the task? Are you going to help us catch the real killer?"

"Yes, sir. One hundred percent. When will DS O'Neill and I join the team in Glasgow?"

"There's no need for that. I've decided to set up the incident room here in Dumbarton," Milligan responded. He could read the surprise on Claire's face and explained. "Dumbarton is closer to where the most recent murder took place and so that's where the freshest evidence and any witnesses will be. You've already set up the incident room, so you, DCI Carter and the rest of his team can get to work right away. I've arranged for the other case files to be transferred to Dumbarton this morning and DCI Mitchell has found me an office to work in while the investigation is on-going."

Claire was impressed by the speed at which all this had been organised – MIT didn't mess about and had access to resources that she could only dream about. She could barely contain her excitement.

Chapter 10

Petrie had become accustomed to the morning routine at the remand unit in Barlinnie: cells for each floor were opened in sequence each morning to stagger and control the influx of hungry men to the dining area. At 8.15 a.m. precisely, it was the turn of the second-floor inmates to go down and eat breakfast before returning to their cells. Today was Monday and therefore once all inmates on the second floor had returned to their cells, the shower routine was initiated. Again, this was organised on a staggered basis to avoid overcrowding in the shower rooms. The large square chambers were furnished with easy-to-clean white wall tiles and chrome showerheads, with a single drain in the centre of the tiled floor. Unlike the walls, the floor tiles were no longer their original bright white and had now worn down to a dirty shade of grey.

Petrie had finished showering and was drying himself off. He put on his fresh prison clothing that had been provided that morning and dumped his dirty clothing in one of the large plastic bins at the end of the shower area. He then made his way up to his cell where those prisoners, who had not yet been allocated cleaning duties, would be given some free time to amuse themselves until the lunchtime rota commenced.

The remand unit in Barlinnie was far more relaxed than the main prison block where the convicted prisoners were held and Petrie felt at ease with his newly acquired daily routine. Mainly because he knew his message had been delivered and he would soon be released as the case against him collapsed.

He strolled back to his two-man cell, casually acknowledging some of the other prisoners on the way. He entered his cell and made his way to his bunk when he suddenly felt a sharp pain in the right-hand side of his lower back and then another. He turned and to his horror he saw Bull standing there, holding the glass knife dripping in blood: his blood! Before Petrie could speak a word Bull stabbed the makeshift knife into Petrie's gut and twisted it, ripping into his stomach, intestines, and anything else it touched. Petrie dropped to his knees. Bull grabbed his head, his huge hand smothering Petrie's mouth, and stabbed Petrie again, this time snapping the blade of the glass.

Petrie fell face down onto the cell floor and lay still. Bull checked the pulse in his neck and was satisfied that Petrie was dead. He then put the handle of the blade in the cell toilet, flushed it and waited to make sure the handle had disappeared. He quickly checked his clothing for obvious bloodstains and noticed a few speckles of blood on his shirt. Confident that they would only be noticed under close inspection, he checked outside the cell before leaving and closed the cell door behind him. A few inmates on the other side of the second-floor corridor saw him exit the cell but that was fine; they had been instructed to keep an eye out for guards and cause a scene if any approached Petrie's cell while Bull carried out his instructions.

Confident that there were no guards around, Bull casually returned to his cell on the first floor, just in time for the prison guards to announce that it was their turn to go to the shower area. Bull joined the crowd heading towards the showers, staying close to the prisoner in front of him. Having made it safely to the shower area, he removed his clothing, rolled them up and dumped them in one of the large bins. He then joined a group of other inmates in the shower room and started to wash himself. The prison alarm sounded as he started to dry himself and then all hell broke out as news of Petrie's death spread throughout the prison.

Chapter 11

DCI Carter called his newly formed team together at 12.30 p.m. to update them on the forensics report which had just been received. He stood in front of the large white incident board, which had now been updated to include information on the two previous deaths. There were also photographs of each of the three victims and other photographs taken at the scenes of each crime fixed to the board, including images of the three identical hammers used to slay the victims.

DCI Carter began his briefing by introducing DI Redding and DS O'Neill to the other members of his team. First, he introduced Detective Sergeant Ramnik Bahanda, known to his colleagues as Rambo. He explained that Rambo was an ICT specialist and would be the go-to person for all matters of a technical nature, especially when it came to the internet and social media but would also assist with digital image analysis.

Carter moved on to introduce Detective Sergeant Ross Greenwood or "Woody" as he was known. Woody would be the Case Manager and would be responsible for the Incident Board and other general administration involved. He would be assisted by two uniformed officers for 'L' Division, PC Brown, and PC Campbell, who had been drafted in to support the investigation, sort evidence, keep the files in order, and where required, kick down doors. Carter informed the team that Claire and Brian would be lead investigators on the Maxwell murder, given their local knowledge and the progress made by Dumbarton CID in eliminating two persons of interest. They would be tasked with interviewing witnesses, taking statements, and so on, and would support DCI Carter, who would oversee the whole investigation as Senior Investigating Officer. Carter would also liaise with the forensics team and supervise the other three DCs from MIT, who had also been assigned to the case; Doyle, Paterson (Patsy) and Montague (Monty).

"Okay, now that we have all been introduced, let's take a look at the forensics received on the Maxwell murder," said Carter, picking up a copy of the report and opening the first page. "First and foremost, the pathologist has confirmed the time of death to be consistent with the statement provided by Robert Baird, Sheila Maxwell's partner. So, we are now confident that she was on the Edinburgh to

Helensburgh train as claimed, but let's get that confirmed by someone else on the same train." Claire noted it down and nodded to Carter to continue.

"So, just to be clear, we think that Sheila Maxwell got off the train at Craigendoran station at approximately 9.42 p.m. and was heading home when she was attacked a few minutes later. The pathologist has also confirmed that the damage inflicted on Sheila Maxwell's skull was consistent with that of damage inflicted on the two other murder victims." Carter pointed to the incident board. That, and the fact that the forensic report confirms that the hammer used was the same make and model as the others, now removes any doubts that we are looking for the same killer for all three murders. Rambo, can you put up the enlarged images of the three hammers on the screen please?"

Within seconds the images appeared on the large monitor on the wall to the left of the incident board. "So, as you can see, we have three identical Stanley hammers with round heads and claws. There are thousands of these sold every year in Scotland from various outlets so impossible to trace. It's highly likely that the killer knows this to be the case."

Claire stood up and approached the screen to take a closer look and then turned to face Carter. "It's as if he wants us to know that he's a serial killer

– using the same weapon and deliberately leaving it behind. Is that normal? I mean for a serial killer?"

"It's a good question and yes, case studies have shown that some serial killers often want their crimes to be known – they want to become as famous as Ted Bundy or the Yorkshire Ripper. Some psychiatrists also believe that some serial killers want to be caught … to be stopped, as they can't help themselves."

"Well, if they want to be caught, why don't they just hand themselves in?" asked Doyle.

There was a rumble of laughter around the room.

"Who knows?" said Carter, ignoring the laughter. "What we do know, given the gaps between the murders and the apparent lack of connection between any of the victims, this one has all the hallmarks of a classic serial killer." He paused to allow that to sink in around the room.

It was a strange feeling for Claire to be on the receiving end of a briefing; she was usually the officer in charge of investigations and felt a bit uneasy. That said, she had been impressed with Carter's assured and confident manner when addressing the team and was keen to participate. "Sir, can I ask one more question about the hammer before we move on?"

"Yes, go ahead."

"Did forensics confirm that the fingerprints on the hammer matched Robert Baird's?"

"I was coming to that. Yes, they did. However, we are satisfied that Baird could not have committed all three murders as he has solid alibis for the first two. Claire, this would be a good opportunity for you to brief the team on Mr Baird's interview. I understand that he gave a reasonable explanation as to why his fingerprints were found on the hammer."

She stood up to address the whole room. "According to Baird, he was so upset at seeing Sheila's battered body lying on the ground, he bent down to comfort her and held her in his arms. That explains the blood on his clothing. However, when he went to lay her down, he claims he lost balance and fell forward at which point his right hand landed on something hard and he automatically picked it up. Realising that the hammer must have been the murder weapon he put it back where he found it."

"And do you believe Baird's version of events, Inspector?" Carter asked, deliberately putting her on the spot.

"Well, he seemed genuinely upset and had no apparent motive, but the evidence was pointing his way until, of course, we were made aware of the other murders. If I may make one comment, sir. Having seen the ferocity of the attack, my gut reaction was that it must be personal and that the attacker knew the victim - he didn't just kill Sheila Maxwell - he absolutely destroyed her. This was why we also interviewed her ex-husband this morning but he also has an alibi – he was at the cinema and…"

"Not to mention the fact that there was no motive - they were divorced years ago and hadn't been in contact," said Carter, interrupting Claire. "Is that correct, Inspector?"

There were a few guffaws in the room and Claire's face reddened. She wanted to slap his face but managed to control herself before responding. "Yes sir, that's correct but we were just being thorough. Leave no stone unturned!"

"Very good, Claire, but now that you have interviewed the ex-husband and established that he has an alibi I think we need to look elsewhere."

"Yes sir, but…"

Carter interrupted her again. "But what? We're wasting time here. We have a dangerous killer at large. Let's move on before I lose my temper."

Claire sat down and was livid. Brian was also seething at how readily Carter had dismissed Claire.

Carter, who appeared to be completely oblivious to the uncomfortable atmosphere in the room, continued with the briefing. "Okay, so we now have three killings with a similar MO. We believe the killer is identifying his victims – middle-aged blondes, at random on the Helensburgh to Edinburgh train line and he likes to use a hammer and leave it at the murder scene. As a starting point, we need to examine all CCTV footage we can get from ScotRail, beginning with the most recent incident in Craigendoran. Monty – that's your responsibility. Who knows, maybe we'll get lucky."

"Yes, boss, but I'll need some support though. That could be a lot of videos to go through."

"Yes, Doyle can assist you," said Carter pointing towards the young DC, the most inexperienced member of the team. Doyle groaned in response – he hated being desk-bound and would much prefer to be out catching the bad guys. Carter ignored his reaction and continued. "Brian, I want you to find out who else was on Sheila Maxwell's train, starting with the ticket inspector and then anyone else in the carriage. I want you to find out if anyone remembers seeing Sheila and whether they noticed anything suspicious or out of the ordinary. We've put out an appeal for witnesses, so hopefully the other passengers will come forward and make your job a bit easier. Patsy will assist you. Any questions?"

"No problem," said Brian, looking round to find Patsy and nodding to him.

"Right, I also want door to door interviews with all the residents whose properties are served by Middleton Lane. Find out if they saw or heard anything unusual last night. Woody, can you get some uniforms to knock on doors, collate their responses and let me know if anything turns up."

"Claire, why don't we go to the crime scene and you can talk me through everything you saw last night? I want to walk the route from the station to where the body was found, get a feel for the area, and see what else we can find."

"Yes sir, it would also be helpful for me and Brian to get sight of the files on the other two cases… to get the full picture. You never know, we might spot something…"

"Something that we missed, is that what you were going to say, Inspector?"

"No, I was going to say - we might spot something which helps us solve the case, sir," she said, quickly covering up her implied criticism.

Carter smiled at the speed with which Claire was able to backtrack and decided to move on. "Right, so let's get busy people. Oh, it goes without saying - we don't want the press to hear that we're looking for a serial killer, so be careful what you say out there. The last thing this investigation needs is a media frenzy."

~

Claire returned to the CID Room to get her coat when her phone buzzed. It was DSup Mulholland from the Regional Organised Crime Team.

"Hello, sir. It's been a while. What's up?"

"Hello, Claire. I take it you haven't heard yet."

"Sorry, heard what, sir?"

"Petrie's dead. He was stabbed in his cell this morning."

Claire was stunned, "What? How did that happen?"

"We don't know yet. I've got a team at Barlinnie investigating but we suspect it's been a hit by another drug gang. This will be news to you, but Petrie was trying to take over the supply of drugs to the Southside before we caught him. We think that's why he had purchased the warehouse in Hillington – it was going to become his main distribution centre on that side of the river. We are working on the theory that a price was put on Petrie's head. It was much easier to get to him in prison than on the outside where he had his gang to protect him. Even with Bull around as protection, they managed to take him out!"

Claire was a little deflated. She was looking forward to the high-profile court case. "So, I suppose that just leaves the case against Bull to be taken to trial?"

"Yes, yes it does, but Claire, that's not the only reason that I'm calling. There's a vacant DI position in the Organised Crime Team – are you interested?"

Chapter 12

Middleton Lane looked quite different in the daylight. The tidy little back lane was lined with sandstone walls, driveways and in some instances, garages. It was obvious to Claire that the area was very affluent: one side of the properties served by Middleton Lane faced the waterfront and so, she knew that those houses must cost a small fortune.

The blue police tape and the incident tent were still in place under the strict instruction of DCI Carter. Some of the house owners had already complained that they couldn't get their cars out as a consequence of his decision but Carter didn't care. He had instructed that every inch of the lane be searched in daylight and so a team of uniformed officers, aided by the SOC team, were slowly and methodically making their way along the lane identifying anything which might require further investigation. So far, they had found nothing of consequence other than a broken street lamp. The broken glass of the lamp had fallen and landed on the ground where it was easily spotted by one member of the search party, who had noted it on the incident log. A SOCO took some photographs of the lamp and the glass below it, and just to be thorough, she took a few samples of the broken glass for testing, even though it was very unlikely that this would be of any use to the investigation.

Claire and Carter entered the tent where Claire described in detail how the body had been found, the position of the hammer and so on. The blood-stained ground had now turned a dark shade of reddish brown as the blood slowly congealed and dried out under the warm lights which had been set up to illuminate the area.

Carter carefully examined the ground. "So, it's possible that Baird's statement fits the scene."

"Yes, there's nothing to suggest otherwise," Claire confirmed.

"Okay, I've seen enough here. I'll take a closer look at the SOCO photographs when I get back to the station. Let's walk the route to the station and back."

They left the tent and continued south towards the station and noticed the broken street lamp.

"I wonder when that happened." Claire pondered.

Carter stopped and looked up at the broken light and rubbed his chin - the overnight stubble beginning to itch a little. "Could be a coincidence, we can get someone to check with the residents. Probably some kids mucking about," he suggested.

"Could be," said Claire. "But look around, it's a good neighbourhood. No sign of litter or any other vandalism for that matter. Let's get the door-to-door team to ask around, just in case."

"No stone unturned?"

Claire nodded. "Exactly."

They walked on through the lane and made their way down towards the dilapidated Craigendoran Pier. It had seen better days and was no longer in use. Claire pointed to a small gate on the left-hand side of the road. "You have to cross over the footbridge to get to the train. There's not any platform on this side of the track."

"Okay, let's do that," said Carter.

They made their way up and over the metal footbridge and down the other side where they could see some passengers standing, waiting for the next train.

Claire stopped suddenly. "Wait a minute! If the killer is picking his victims on the train at random, as we now suspect, then he must be using the train to get back home. He wouldn't have any other form of transport available to him."

Carter also stopped to consider this. "You're right, and if he used the train to return home from here, he must have come back this way."

Claire looked around the platform and spotted the CCTV cameras mounted high on the steel stanchions. "There!" she said, pointing up the set of cameras facing the footbridge. "There's a good chance we'll catch him coming down the steps, face forward." She took out her phone, quickly opened the Trainline app and started scrolling down the train times. "Right, the next train to leave Craigendoran heading to Edinburgh was 9.58 p.m. It's tight but he could have made it."

Carter nodded. "Yes, assuming that he was heading back in that direction and not going on to the end of the line."

Claire agreed. "Well, it's a half-hourly service so the next train heading to Helensburgh would be, let's see, yes it would be 10.12 p.m. So, we now think that he either got the 9.58 p.m. or 10.12 p.m. train back home. Either way, that camera would have captured him coming down the stairs to the platform."

"Right, let's get Monty onto ScotRail and get the CCTV footage from that camera. It's got to be our best chance of getting a good look at our killer."

Claire laughed. "Oh yeah, by the way, who comes up with the silly nicknames for the team?"

"Well, unless it's obvious, I usually have the final say, otherwise some of the suggested names might be considered offensive."

"So, what about me, then?" she asked.

"Well, you are second in charge so it's either Ma'am or boss as far as the rest of the team is concerned but I'm happy to stick with Claire unless you have something else in mind."

"Oh no, Claire is fine but what about Brian?"

"What do you call him?"

"Just Brian, the rest of my team call him 'Sarge'."

"Yeah well, that won't work with two other sergeants in the team so we'll just need to come up with something appropriate, won't we? How about Brains? It's an anagram."

"I think he'd prefer to stick with just Brian," said Claire.

"How good is he anyway? Do you rate him?" asked Carter.

"Let's put it this way. I wouldn't be here if it wasn't for his quick thinking, so yes, I rate him. But he's much more than that. He's loyal, dependable, and his local knowledge of this area has been invaluable to me. We would never have caught the Keeper without him."

"Oh, yes, I remember that case. Didn't do your reputation any harm either?" he said, grinning to himself.

The two detectives crossed over the footbridge and walked slowly back towards Middleton Lane, both pleased that they had uncovered another line of enquiry. They passed the line of uniformed officers walking towards them – the officers' eyes focussed on the ground below, looking for the smallest of clues to catch the killer.

Claire broke the brief moment of silence. "So, how many serial killer cases have you worked on, sir?"

"Just the one before this," Carter replied. "They're quite rare in this part of the world," he added.

Claire was surprised by this, especially after the sharp remarks made by DSup Milligan. She had expected the DCI to be a bit more experienced than that and Carter could sense that Claire was chewing this over. "Go on, Inspector. Let's hear what's on your mind?"

"Sorry, it's just that I got the impression that you had a bit more experience than the one case."

"Well, as I said, we don't get many cases of serial killers in Scotland but psychopaths... well ... we've got plenty of them to go around and I've had my fair share of those cases."

"Ah, I see," said Claire. "Do you think our killer is a psychopath?"

"It's hard to say until we get him locked up, but one thing is for certain - there does seem to be a lot of anger involved in these killings. It might be helpful if we speak to our psychiatric profiler about this case. We have an arrangement with Professor Charlene Tannock, at Glasgow University – we let her interview the psychopaths that we catch for her research, and in turn, she gives free profiling advice on our ongoing cases."

"A mutualistic symbiotic relationship," said Claire in response.

"What?" Carter asked, slightly bemused by her strange observation.

"Where two separate organisms benefit each other – it's a biological term used to describe animal life that helps each other - like with clownfish and sea anemones; the clownfish feed on the small invertebrates that harm the anemones and the anemones help the clownfish hide from their predators, and so they both benefit," she explained.

"Yes, something like that… anyway, leave it with me and I'll set up the meeting – I'm sure she'll be interested in this case."

"I'm looking forward to it," said Claire. "We don't get access to that type of resource in poor old CID."

"I know," said Carter. "I remember when I first started – having to wait days for forensic reports, even longer for technical support and analysis. Well, you're in MIT now, Claire, and top priority is a given."

Claire smiled. "Yes, I do believe I could get used to this."

Chapter 13

Back at the station, Brian and Patsy had tracked down the ticket inspector and had called him in for an interview. Ronald McColl, a rotund ginger-haired man in his late forties, wearing his ScotRail uniform, with an ill-fitting shirt hanging out below his jacket, arrived at the station right on time and after a brief delay was taken up to Interview Room 2 by PC Campbell. Brian and Patsy were sitting waiting and stood up to welcome him when he entered the room.

Ronald McColl, who had a mild heart condition, chose to keep his facemask on during the interview. As a further precaution, the seats were placed two metres apart as per the COVID guidance. It had been a complete nightmare throughout the lockdown when the masks were mandatory but after the first set of vaccines had been rolled out, the rules had been relaxed a little.

After a brief introduction and much to McColl's relief, Brian assured him that he was only there to help the police with the enquiry and was not a suspect.

Brian removed a recent photograph of Sheila Maxwell from the folder in front of him and slid it across the table to Mr McColl. "Mr McColl, I would like you to take a good look at this photograph and tell me if you remember seeing this woman on the train last night. She would have got on the Edinburgh to Helensburgh train at Haymarket and got off the train at Craigendoran, at approximately 9.42 p.m."

McColl took a good look at the photograph. "Yes, I think I did see her. Quite an attractive blonde for her age. I think she may have been in the last carriage but couldn't be sure."

Brian was pleased that McColl had responded so positively and continued with the questioning. "Right … good. So, do you remember if there was anyone else in the same carriage with her?

"Not with her. I'm fairly sure she was sitting on her own but there could have been others in the same carriage… in fact, I'm fairly sure there was," he said, staring up at the ceiling, peering into the deep recesses of his memory.

"Can you describe what she was wearing?" asked Brian.

"If my memory serves me correctly, she was wearing a dark green coat. Looked like wool. Oh, and she had a handbag... black leather, I think."

"Anything else?" Brian prompted.

"No, sorry."

Brian continued. "Now think very carefully, Mr McColl. Think back to the carriage. Try to visualise who was in there with this woman. Now, can you describe them?"

McColl took his time, sat back, crossed his arms and stared up at the ceiling again. "Yes, I think there might have been a couple of men. I can't describe their faces as both had their facemasks on but one had a long dark coat, it might have been navy blue or black. I only noticed it because I had been thinking of getting something similar for myself. Oh, and I think he was wearing trainers which was a bit weird. Some people have no dress sense."

Brian looked the dishevelled ticket inspector up and down and then held back from making any comment. During the short pause, something suddenly occurred to Patsy. "Mr McColl, you said both men in the carriage were wearing facemasks. Was Mrs Maxwell also wearing a facemask?"

McColl's face lit up. "Yes, I remember now. She was wearing a facemask but had to remove it to open her phone."

The two police officers turned to each other, both sharing the same bewildered look of confusion. McColl could see he had lost them and explained further, "She used face recognition to open her phone … to show her electronic ticket to me. That's how I recognised her even though she had a facemask."

McColl sat there extremely pleased with himself but not as pleased as the two detectives sitting opposite.

Brian nodded. "Right, so thinking back to this man in the long coat. I know you didn't see his face properly but can you remember his hair colour, eye colour, anything at all?"

"Sorry, I think he had dark hair but as for his eye colour… nope, sorry."

"What about his height or build?"

"Hard to say as he was seated but I reckon he was taller than me judging by the length of his legs. Not sure about the build – probably medium. Again, he was wearing a coat so it was hard to tell."

Brian continued. "And the other man? Remember anything – long hair, short hair? A beard or a moustache…"

McColl suddenly remembered. "Oh! Yes, I remember now. He did have a beard. I couldn't see it properly because of the mask but I could see under his chin. Oh! And I think he was also going a bit thin on top."

"Right. That's good. Anything else? Do you remember what he was wearing? What about his build?"

"No, not really," McColl replied, "But I think he was the same height as me – about 5 foot 9, and maybe of medium build... I think. Sorry, I'm not much help, am I?"

"That's okay Mr McColl. You've been extremely helpful." Brian turned towards his colleague. "Any further questions?"

Patsy looked surprised to be asked and quickly shook his head. "Nope."

"Okay then, Mr McColl. Thanks for all your help." Brian took a small business card out of his jacket pocket and handed it to the ticket inspector. "If you remember anything else, anything at all, please give me a call. And thanks again for coming in so quickly."

Patsy stood up. "Come on then Mr McColl. I'll take you down to the exit."

McColl followed Patsy out of the room while Brian picked up the folder and returned to the incident room. Woody was sitting in the corner of the room, logging the evidence bags from the Craigendoran site, which had been returned by the SOCO. Brian went over to the board and started to scribble down a few notes when a thought occurred to him. *Where's the facemask?* "Woody, where's the list of items that were found on Sheila Maxwell?" he asked.

Woody pointed to a row of folders on a shelf near the window. "It should be in the second folder from the left ... the black one."

Brian found the folder and started to go through it until he found the list. He scanned it, looking to see if the facemask was there – it wasn't. *Thought so.* He took out his mobile phone and called Claire.

~

Claire was sitting in her car, checking messages on her phone when it rang. She recognised the number and answered without delay, "Hello Brian, what's up?"

"Hi boss, I've just finished interviewing the train inspector and got a positive ID on Sheila Maxwell. She was on the train as Baird claimed. And, we may have a rough description of the killer provided he was in the same carriage as Sheila Maxwell - there were only two men in the same carriage so one of them could be our killer."

"That's great Brian. I'll let the DCI know. Oh, you should know that we're confident that we'll be able to get a good view of the killer from the overhead CCTV at Craigendoran station. The DCI is speaking to Monty about arranging for the recording to be sent over to the station."

"That's great boss, but not the only reason why I'm calling - the Ticket Inspector said that Sheila was wearing a facemask, but there's not one logged on the list of items provided by the SOCO."

Claire knew right away what Brian was thinking. "So, you think the killer might be taking souvenirs?"

"Wouldn't be the first time… would it?" said Brian.

"No, you're right, but she may have dropped it outside the train by accident or put it in a bin. I'm forever losing mine. If she did drop it on the street, the search team will find it. They're working their way towards the station now. Well done, Brian."

Claire ended the call and got out of her car. She found the sergeant leading the search team and told him to look out for the facemask. Finally, she then went looking for Carter to share the news. *Things were looking up.*

Chapter 14

Claire arrived back at the station, full of enthusiasm. She knew that the camera at Craigendoran station was their best chance of getting a positive ID of the killer but was also pleased with the progress made by Brian and Patsy.

She entered the busy incident room to be greeted by Brian. "Hello, boss. That was quick," he commented.

"I was keen to get back as soon as possible. Have we got the CCTV footage yet?"

"Not yet. Monty's been onto ScotRail and has requested it as a matter of urgency. Where's Carter?" he asked, looking beyond Claire to see if the DCI was following her.

"He's not far behind me. He had to take a call from DSup Milligan - probably looking for an update on our progress," she explained.

"Well, in that case, I may as well give you the full notes on our interview with Mr McColl, the ticket inspector."

Claire walked over to the incident board. "Ah, yes. So, what do we know?"

"Right, we know that one of the two men was wearing a long dark coat, possibly navy blue or black. He was wearing a facemask so we don't have a description of his face but the ticket inspector, Mr. Ronald McColl, thinks that he had dark hair. He also thinks that the man in the long coat was wearing trainers."

Claire mulled that over. "Okay, and the other passenger?"

"Well, we don't have too much to go on but he had a beard underneath his facemask and was going slightly thin on top."

"Clothing?"

"Nope, he couldn't remember anything about what the guy was wearing."

"Right then. Well, the CCTV footage should tell us if either of the two men got off the train at Craigendoran and followed Sheila Maxwell. They would need to cross over the footbridge but more importantly, Carter and I both think the killer would need to return by the footbridge to get the next train home, wherever that may be."

Brian nodded in agreement.

Claire had another thought. "What about the CCTV on the train? Are we also getting a copy of that?"

Brian shook his head. "We've checked. They don't record the CCTV on trains – they only provide live images to help the driver spot any trouble on the train."

"Really, what is the point of that?" asked Claire.

"I know," said Brian. "But at least we'll get the CCTV from the station ..."

Brian was interrupted by the ringing of the phone in the far corner of the incident room and looked around to see if anyone would pick it up.

PC Brown was the first to react. He took the message and relayed it to Brian and Claire. "It's the desk sergeant. He says there's a man down at reception who claims to have been on the train with Sheila Maxwell last night. Apparently, he recognised her from the photo published in the media release."

"Right, go down and bring him up, please. Brian, we'll do the interview. Woody – can you let the DCI know as soon as he gets in, please?"

"Will do Claire – I mean… ma'am.'

Claire smiled. "Woody, you can call me anything you like, but not ma'am. Got it."

"Right, well it will need to be Claire then, as Carter is the boss."

Brian was about to say something impolite in return but Claire quickly intervened. "Right, come on Brian, let's go and speak to our mystery witness."

Chapter 15

The witness, Leonard Harkness, was escorted up to the interview room where Claire and Brian were already seated and waiting for him. They introduced themselves, thanked him for coming and then took note of his full name, address, telephone number and other details before starting the questioning. It was obvious to both detectives that Harkness, who had decided to keep his facemask on during the interview, fitted the description provided by the ticket inspector - ginger thin hair and beard - but Claire was nevertheless determined to be very thorough and not make any assumptions.

"So, Mr Harkness, I understand that you recognised Sheila Maxwell from the photograph issued in our press release and you believe you were on the same train as her last night. Is that correct?"

"Yes, that's correct," he said.

"Good. Which carriage were you on?"

"I think it was the last carriage."

"And who else was in the carriage with you?"

"Well, there was the woman in the photo, Sheila Maxwell, and another bloke."

Claire and Brian exchanged a quick look but kept a poker face.

"Can you describe this... other bloke?" asked Claire.

Harkness paused a little to gather his thoughts. "He was wearing a facemask so I didn't get a good look at his face but I think he was wearing a dark coat."

"What about his hair colour - can you remember if it was blonde or…"

"It was dark, maybe dark brown – I don't think it was black."

"Good," said Claire encouragingly. "Now, I know you did not get a good look at his face but how old do you think this man was?

Brian winced a little. He hadn't asked that question of the ticket inspector and was silently kicking himself.

"Oh, em, maybe in his late forties. I couldn't be sure."

"That's okay, Mr. Harkness. You're doing well. Can you describe his build and height?

"Well, he looked to be of medium build. Again, I'm not one hundred percent on that and, as for his height, well, I think he must have been about 6 ft. Taller than me, anyway."

"How can you be so sure?" Brian asked, determined to improve on his previous performance when interviewing the ticket inspector. "After all, he was sitting down… I assume"

Harkness hesitated a little before speaking. "He was seated, but he stood up to get off the train at Craigendoran."

Claire and Brian almost burst with excitement. "You actually saw him get off the train at Craigendoran?" asked Claire.

"Yes, I stayed on the train and got off at Helensburgh Central," he responded.

"Did you walk home from the station?" asked Claire.

"No, my wife was waiting to give me a lift. We live up by the Hill House – too far for me to walk. I have a dodgy knee thanks to an old rugby injury."

"Thank you, Mr Harkness. If I can take you back to the train again. Where were you sitting in relation to the other passengers?" asked Claire.

"I was sitting in the back of the carriage, facing the direction of travel – I don't like travelling backwards. Sheila Maxwell was sitting on the opposite side from me with her back to the direction of travel and the other bloke was sitting two rows of seats directly behind her, facing the same direction."

"Right, so you could see both of them but Mrs Maxwell could only see you, is that correct?"

"Yes, that's correct," he said, failing to notice the significance of the question.

"Was Mrs Maxwell wearing a facemask?" asked Brian.

"Yes, it was one of the flowery patterned ones – made of cloth."

Another detail that Brian had omitted to ask the ticket inspector, but he was determined to be more thorough this time round. "Right, so how can you be sure that it was Sheila Maxwell if she was wearing a facemask the whole time?"

"She removed her mask when the ticket inspector asked to see her ticket," he responded quickly, having anticipated the follow-up question.

Brian smiled and turned towards Claire to show that he had now finished that line of questioning.

"Thank you, Mr Harkness. I've just a few more questions and then you can get on your way," said Claire. "You said that you saw both Sheila Maxwell and the other passenger leave the train at Craigendoran station. Can you remember who left the carriage first?"

"I think it was Mrs Maxwell. Yes, I'm fairly sure it was her - the man in the long coat got up and held the upper handrail and didn't leave the carriage until the door opened. That's when I noticed how tall he was."

"And did you see where Sheila Maxwell went after she left the train?" Claire asked.

Harkness looked confused so Claire expanded the question. "Did she head towards the tunnel or the footbridge?"

"Oh, I see what you mean. Sorry, I can't remember."

"And the other man, did you see which way he went?" she continued.

"Sorry, I didn't notice… wait, do you think, the other man… that he might be the killer?"

Claire and Brian could not believe it had taken this long for the penny to drop.

"Right now, we have no evidence to suggest that the other passenger was anything more than just that – another passenger," said Brian. "I have one final question though. Did you notice anything unusual about this man's clothing or footwear?"

"No, sorry. I don't think I looked down at his feet."

Claire was grateful that Brian had remembered to ask the question, even though the answer was negative. "Thanks again for coming in Mr Harkness, you have been most helpful. However, we will need to speak to your wife to confirm your statement and may need to call you back for further questioning, if necessary, is that okay?" asked Claire.

"Call me back! But I thought this interview would be sufficient," he said anxiously.

"It's okay, Mr Harkness. There's no need to be concerned," said Brian, reassuringly. "Now, if you will follow me, I'll take you down to the exit."

~

Brian escorted Harkness downstairs while Claire headed back to the incident room. DCI Carter and DC Doyle were sitting together looking at Doyle's screen. Claire approached them and could see the video they were looking at was from Craigendoran station. Carter's facial expression was not one of joyful happiness.

"I see you got the CCTV footage – that was quick," said Claire.

Carter turned towards her. "Oh! Hi Claire. Yes, we got it but there's a problem."

"Oh? What's wrong?"

"The fucking CCTV camera, the one pointing towards the footbridge, was down … is down and has been for four fuckin' days. Bloody ScotRail – useless bunch of…"

"Wait look, boss," said Monty excitedly pointing to his screen. He had been reviewing the footage from some of the other cameras. "Camera 4 is also pointing at the footbridge. It's further away but we should be able to see something."

Monty moved the video on to 9.40 p.m., as Carter and Claire crouched beside him to get a better view of the small screen.

"Wait, can you project it onto the big screen so we can all get a better look?" said Claire.

Before Monty could respond, Rambo came over and looked at the connections. "Two minutes, I have an extended HDMI lead in my bag." He ran over to his laptop case, got the lead and connected it from Monty's laptop to the big screen, just in time for Brian to enter the room.

"What's going on?" asked Brian.

"CCTV footage of Craigendoran station," said Claire. "Pull up a chair, Brian, this is going to be good." She turned to Carter. "Sir, we're looking for a white male, medium build, approximately 6 ft tall, dark hair and wearing a long dark coat."

"Your witness?" asked Carter, directing his question to Brian.

"Two witnesses," Brian replied. "The train inspector and another passenger gave a similar description of a third passenger who got off the train at Craigendoran."

"Right," said Carter. "Let's see what we've got then."

The room fell silent as Monty ran the video. All eyes in the room stared at the big screen, full of expectation - desperate to get their first view of the main suspect. According to the digital clock on the top left-hand side of the screen, the train arrived at the station at 21:43:02. All eyes looked to the last carriage. After a short delay, the doors opened.

"That's Sheila Maxwell," shouted Doyle, as if he was the only one in the room who recognised her. Carter ignored his youthful enthusiasm.

"She's still wearing her mask," said Claire towards Carter, who nodded acknowledging the significance of the observation.

"There he is," said Doyle. "Long coat!" The camera caught a glimpse of the man's profile before he turned and headed for the footbridge. Unfortunately, the quality of the image was poor; the station was dark and the camera was too far away to reveal any details.

"He's still wearing his mask," Claire pointed out.

They watched the video until both Sheila Maxwell and the man were out of sight.

"Right, well, we've not got a lot to work with there, but at least we know he headed in the same direction as the victim. What was the time of the next train, Claire?" asked Carter, who was keen to move on.

"It would be the 9.58 p.m. – the train to Edinburgh."

"Right, Monty let's run the video quickly and stop whenever we see anyone come down the footbridge."

Doyle did as he was instructed. The digital clock moved quickly through the minutes until Doyle caught sight of the 9.58 train arriving.

"Nothing boss," said Doyle.

"Okay. We weren't sure if he would make that one. It would have been a very quick turn-around," said Carter, trying to sound positive but failing to hide the disappointment on his face. Okay, let's run the video on again. Claire – what's the next train time? "

"That would be the 10.12 pm train to Helensburgh," she replied.

"Right, Monty. Let's go," said Carter, this time a little less patiently than before. Everyone in the room could sense that his earlier good mood was slowly dissipating.

The video sped on through the minutes, and again Monty stopped it when the train arrived."

"What the fuck!" Carter shouted in anger. "Where the fuck is he?"

The room was silent. No one wanted to be the first to speak. Claire was deep in thought. She was convinced that he must have returned by train but clearly, she had been wrong.

Carter composed himself and addressed the room. "Right, he may not have returned via the footbridge so Monty… and Doyle, I want you two to go through all the video again, this time checking all cameras and the entrance to the tunnel and do it in real-time."

"Yes, boss," they replied together.

"Rambo, get a copy of the video and focus on the image of the suspect, just as he left the train. I know it's dark and he was backlit by the lights of the train but see what you can do to enhance it."

"I'll do my best boss but he was quite a distance away from the camera and he was wearing a facemask," Rambo replied.

Carter ignored the response and moved on. "Woody, once Rambo has done his job, get the image and a description of our suspect over to the British Transport Police and instruct them to let us know as soon as there are any sightings. And make sure they know he could be dangerous. Claire, Brian - I want a detailed briefing on your interviews with the two witnesses on my desk, as soon as possible. Milligan is on his way here and I need to have some good news to give him!"

Chapter 16

Ever since Petrie's arrest, McCafferty used the office above the pub to conduct any *confidential business* which needed to be done out of earshot of the nosy bar staff; they had no clue about the huge drug deals which were taking place just a few feet above their heads. That was, until news of Petrie's arrest spread rapidly throughout social media, quickly followed by the national media, which always seemed to be a step behind its modern rival. Some of the more discerning staff chose to leave when discovering the truth about their employer, but others, who liked to be associated with the notoriety of working for a famous gangster stayed and were now keen to listen to and spread every little rumour circulating the pub like a virus - the wider it spread, the more the rumour changed until it would appear as a new variant of what might have once been something close to the truth. This was how legends were made and how evil, vicious, twisted gangsters like Petrie would become celebrated over time. However, news of Petrie's demise had not yet filtered down to the masses but would soon enough.

On receiving Petrie's instruction to have DI Redding killed, McCafferty had done as requested and now the matter was out of his hands. The money had been transferred to an offshore account as instructed by the assassin and therefore it was only a matter of time before the target would be found and killed. McCafferty could have used one of Petrie's men to do the hit but knew that Petrie did not want this. The sum mentioned in the instruction was clearly high enough to pay for a professional; someone who could not be linked directly to Petrie. No, Petrie knew what he was doing.

McCafferty was sitting in Petrie's office, staring out of the window, wondering how the assassin would deal with DI Redding. He jumped a little when his mobile phone started to ring. He looked at the screen and could see that it was Petrie's solicitor, Wallace.

"Mr McCafferty, I'm afraid I have some bad news," said Wallace.

McCafferty could tell that the man was rattled. "Oh, what's happened?"

"Petrie's dead. He was stabbed to death in his cell."

"Jesus Christ! Do they know who killed him?" asked McCafferty, his mind struggling to understand the enormity of what he had just been told.

"No, but the police are investigating it. I have been told that the Organised Crime Team are involved so it looks like they think that it was gang-related."

"Baxter?"

"Possibly, I don't know."

"Shit! So, what do I do now? What happens to the pub?"

"Well, it will take some time to resolve, so just keep operating as normal."

"And the other business?" McCafferty asked.

"My advice is to walk away. Leave it to Baxter or some other gangster to take over."

While McCafferty was thinking about the implications of the solicitor's advice, Wallace took the opportunity to address the issue that he had actually called about. He chose his words carefully. "It goes without saying … now that Mr. Petrie is dead, his previous request is no longer required."

McCafferty took a deep inhale of breath. "It's too late."

"What do you mean it's too late?" Wallace responded, his voice reaching a higher octave.

"The request has been issued."

"Can't you cancel the request?" asked Wallace, whose heart was now beginning to race.

"It doesn't work like that. Look, I think we had better have this conversation in person. You never know who might be listening."

Wallace froze. "What? Oh… right, yes. Let's do that." He hung up the phone quickly and wiped the sweat from his furrowed brow. He sat there thinking … *what did I say?* After a minute or so he calmed himself down, confident that he had not said anything which could be linked to the murder of DI Redding but still wasn't happy that it couldn't be stopped. He started to think like a lawyer again. Even if he had said something which could be used against him and the police had bugged McCafferty's phone – warrant or no warrant, he would get the whole conversation thrown out of court, as it would be a breach of solicitor-client confidentiality. After all, he was only calling to offer advice – that was his job.

Chapter 17

It was 6 p.m. by the time Brian made his way home to his three-bedroom terraced house in High Mains Avenue, Dumbarton. It had been an exceptionally long day and he was completely knackered. He entered the hallway, took off his coat and hung it up on the white wooden coat rack on his right. "Agnes… are you home, love?" There was no response which was a wee bit strange as Agnes was usually in the kitchen making dinner at this time in the evening. She was a creature of habit. He popped his head into the small living room to see if she was there and then headed upstairs.

"Hello? Agnes!" he called again and then walked into their bedroom.

Agnes was lying on the bed, weeping. "What's the matter, love?" he asked, his heart sinking a little.

She pointed to the letter which was lying open on the bedside cabinet. Brian knew it was bad news. "The biopsy results?" His heart sank a little bit further and his stomach began to churn.

Agnes nodded and pushed herself upright on the bed, her back resting on the soft upholstered headboard. Brian picked up the letter and read it slowly; trying to take in every word, looking for any glimmer of hope. The letter confirmed his worst fears: the biopsies were positive – Agnes had cancer in both breasts.

"It says you should call the clinic for further information," he said. "It may not be as bad as you think, love. They can perform miracles these days." He said the words but without any real conviction.

Agnes looked up at him and more tears started to stream down her cheeks. "I called them earlier… it's… it's stage four, Brian."

Brian was no expert but he knew that stage four was as serious as it gets. He bent down, hugged Agnes and started to cry. After a few minutes, she gently pushed him away.

She wiped the tears from her face and then used her thumbs to rub the tears from his cheeks. "I've to go in for a double mastectomy and then it's a course of chemotherapy," she said.

"Right. That's good. They obviously think you have a chance if that's what they're recommending?"

Agnes nodded. She didn't have the heart to tell him that the 5-year survival rate for metastatic patients was roughly 20 percent. So, yes, she had a chance, albeit the odds were against her. She had always been the stronger of the two when it came to emotional upset - Brian might be the big, tough policeman on the outside but deep down inside he was a softie, and she knew that she would need to be brave and keep a positive outlook for his sake. She had shed her tears and the worst part, telling Brian, was over. She smiled up at the man that she had loved ever since they had met at college all those years ago. "You're right, love. There's life in this old dog yet but I'm really not looking forward to the chemotherapy - I hear it can be hellish!"

He looked concerned. "But you are still going to go through with it... after the operation?"

"Yes, love. Of course, I will." She stood up, kissed him on the cheek and composed herself. "Right then, what do you want for dinner? I have chicken or chicken," she quipped.

"Chicken, it is then!" he said with more enthusiasm than was necessary and then followed her downstairs to the kitchen.

Chapter 18

As soon as Claire got home, she told Peter all about her being assigned to MIT and the progress they were making tracking down the Craigendoran killer. As always, he listened with interest and said the right words in the right places but deep down he was concerned that she was now chasing a killer. *She was pregnant, after all!*

After dinner, they went through to the living room and sat on their favourite sofa, directly in front of the television. Peter automatically picked up the remote control to turn the television on. "Can we have a chat first?" asked Claire. She knew that as soon as the TV was on the conversation would dry up.

"Sure, what about?"

"I've had a job offer and I'm not sure what to do about it."

"A job offer?" asked Peter. She had his full attention now.

"Do you remember when I told you about Detective Superintendent Mulholland? You know, when I went after Petrie."

Peter stiffened at the sound of Petrie's name. "Yes … I think so."

"Well, he offered me a chance to work for him in the Organised Crime Team in Glasgow."

Peter hesitated before responding and chose his words carefully. "That's great Claire, but isn't it a bit dangerous? I mean, you were hurt bringing in Petrie and…"

Claire could see where Peter was going with this and cut him off. "It's okay, I haven't made up my mind yet and to be honest, I think my talents sit better with MIT - chasing killers."

This comment did not make Peter feel any better and Claire could see that he was getting more anxious with every word she spoke. "Don't worry, Peter, I'm now part of a team of large, strapping men who will do all the rough work, when required. I won't be going anywhere or doing anything on my own, anytime soon. Remember, according to the pregnancy risk assessment, I've to avoid any situation which puts me or the baby at risk. Oh, and I almost forgot to tell you. You'll never guess what Mulholland also told me - Petrie's been killed, while in prison. It's a pity as I was looking forward to the trial."

Peter didn't know how to react. Part of him was relieved that the nightmare was over, another part of him was numb with fear. "How was he killed? I mean, do they know who did it?"

"No, but they think it was another crime gang. Petrie had a lot of enemies."

"I bet he did," said Peter. "So, I suppose this means that you won't need to give any evidence at trial?"

"Not against Petrie… obviously, but there's still one of his henchmen in jail - a big brute of a man called Bull. So, yes, there will be a trial."

"Oh! Right," said Peter. "I thought if Petrie was dead, it would be over."

"Well, it is for Petrie," joked Claire.

Peter wasn't smiling.

Chapter 19

Carter had arranged to meet with Professor Tannock at 9 a.m. in her office at Glasgow University. She had a lecture scheduled for 10 a.m. and therefore was not able to make the trip to Dumbarton to speak to the detectives about their latest case. Carter led the way up the narrow sandstone staircase to the professor's office - a journey he had made several times before. He knocked on the heavy wooden door and entered.

"Good morning, James. It's lovely to see you again," said Professor Tannock, rising from her chair to greet her guests. "And this must be the famous DI Redding, who killed my former colleague, Professor William Fairbairn-Smythe. You're a lot smaller and prettier than I had imagined."

Claire was completely dumbstruck by the remark. She had forgotten that 'the Keeper' had worked at Glasgow University and therefore would have known Professor Tannock. "I'm sorry if …" said Claire apologetically, unsure what to say.

"Oh, don't be sorry dear. He was a pompous arsehole. You did us all a favour," said Tannock smiling, and shook Claire's hand. "It's a pleasure to meet you, detective."

Claire knew that she was going to like Professor Tannock. The middle-aged woman with bright red curly hair was wearing just about every colour under the rainbow; a bright yellow neck scarf, a blue blouse, a deep pink cardigan, a purple Paisley patterned skirt, thick green tights, and shiny red shoes. She was not what Claire was expecting at all, but Claire had to admire her colourful style and her rumbustious personality.

"Please, do have a seat and tell me all about your latest killer," said Tannock excitedly.

Claire noticed that the Professor had a soft English accent and reckoned there was a clear hint of the southwest, maybe Dorset or Cornwall, in her voice. Claire, who was far too polite to ask, decided that she would do a background search on the Professor when she returned to the office.

Carter made himself comfortable and then gave a very concise summary of everything the police knew about the killer so far.

Professor Tannock listened carefully and took some notes. She waited for Carter to finish before speaking. "Well, it does appear that your killer has all the classic traits of a serial killer and therefore is likely to kill again but you know that already and what you are really here for is for me to give you a mental picture of the type of person you are after. Am I correct?"

Claire spoke before Carter could respond. "Yes, if there are any particular personality traits which we should be looking out for with this type of psychopath."

"Yes, detective. I have had the good fortune to interview and study a number of psychopaths and the one thing that they all have in common is that they are all quite different."

Carter knew that would be the Professor's initial response to the question but also knew there was more to follow - otherwise, he would not have made the trip to Glasgow.

The professor continued speaking. "As for personality traits. Well, it depends on who you read. Let's see." She turned to the bookshelf on her right and started to take out book after book. "You see, even the most distinguished experts on the subject can't quite agree." She picked up each of the books in turn. "So, there is Eysenck's Model of Personality, which incorporates Hippocrates' four temperaments but that's only the starting point. Then there's Allport, of course, and then Cattell's sixteen primary personality factors. Oh, yes, we have Tupes and Christal, who succeeded in reducing Cattell's traits down to five recurring factors but the one I favour most is Cleckley." She reached over to the bookshelf and removed a small leather-bound book and opened it. "You see, Cleckley provides a range of traits which most psychopaths have displayed when subjected to scrutiny, so let's start there, shall we?"

Claire nodded in agreement, eager to hear more.

"Fundamentally, Cleckley suggests that most psychopaths are intelligent but have a poverty of emotions; they have no sense of shame and are often egocentric. Some have a superficial charm – you would never guess that they were psychopaths if you lived with them, worked with them, or even socialised with them. Cleckley's studies also showed that most psychopaths lack any sense of guilt and do not suffer from any level of anxiety which gives them an in-built immunity to punishment. And, if that is not bad enough, they can also be unpredictable, irresponsible, and manipulative which makes them extremely dangerous and exceedingly difficult to catch. Isn't that right James?"

Carter nodded. "Difficult, but not impossible. And this one wants us to know that he's a serial killer – leaving the murder weapon behind, using the same make and model of hammer every time, identifying and pursuing his victims on the train. It's as if he's daring us to catch him."

"And yet, you haven't," Tannock responded.

"Professor, these murders were particularly brutal in nature," said Claire. "They looked personal to me but the victims are clearly unconnected other than in appearance. What does that suggest to you?"

"Oh James, you do have a bright one here," said Tannock. "That's a good question, detective. Firstly, a psychopath does not need there to be a personal connection or even personal reason to commit a brutal murder. But, there have been numerous occasions on record when the initial seed or motivation to kill has been linked to a particularly traumatic childhood or adult experience. Your killer does appear to be targeting a certain kind of female and please correct me if I'm wrong – middle-aged, attractive, blonde, so it seems likely that this is the trigger. It could have been a teacher he hated at school, a mother, a daughter, a wife, a partner, a lover, a girlfriend, or any female who has had a negative impact on the killer at some stage in his life."

"So, it's possible that the killer, this psychopath, could be connected to one of our known victims?" asked Claire.

"Yes, it's possible."

"And he's likely to strike again?"

"Yes."

"And what else can you tell us about our killer based on what we've shared with you, Alexis?" asked Carter.

"Well, you're probably looking for a white, heterosexual middle-aged man, well-educated, possibly professional but also familiar with tools; you know, someone who is good at fixing or making things with his hands. He would undoubtedly like to keep himself fit and may attend a local gym. It's also likely that he will commute to work given his use of trains to target his victims."

Claire was impressed. Carter hadn't mentioned anything about the man in the long coat to the Professor and although they couldn't get a decent image of his face from the CCTV, he certainly dressed like he was middle-aged and appeared lean and strong, so the gym reference seemed to make sense.

"Anything else?" pressed Carter.

"Not with what you've given me so far but give me full access to your file and I'll work up a detailed profile," she replied, knowing full well what the response would be.

"Sorry, but I'm not authorised to share anything else with you at the moment. We're trying to keep a tight lid on things. The press doesn't know there's a serial killer on the loose yet and…"

Tannock interrupted Carter. "I hate to break the news to you detective but the lid has just blown off that particular tin!"

"What do you mean?" he asked.

"The Daily Record has just posted it and it's gone viral."

Both detectives pulled out their phones and immediately searched for the Daily Record, and there it was: 'Police Scotland hunt serial killer.' Carter clicked on the link which took him to the article. The headline was 'Hammer Horror.' "Christ, they even know about the murder weapon. How the fuck did they get that piece of information?"

"Well, James, if I were a betting woman, I would guess that you have a leak somewhere in your team. Now, if we're finished, I need to prepare for my next lecture."

Claire and Carter thanked Professor Tannock for her help and made their way back to the car.

"She's right, you know. Someone has leaked it," said Carter. "And if I catch the bastard, they're fuckin' history."

"Who would be so stupid? They must know that it will be traced back to them … eventually."

"You're right and when I get back to the station, I'm putting Woody on the case to do just that. Christ almighty, Milligan is going to have a fit and a bad turn."

"I take it he's not the type to take bad news well," said Claire.

"You can say that again. I fully expect him to rip me out a new arsehole when we get back!"

Chapter 20

You could cut the atmosphere in the incident room with a knife. Carter and Claire had returned to the station and within minutes Milligan appeared and summoned Carter to his makeshift office, which was conveniently located further along the corridor.

Claire looked around the room and noticed that Brian was sitting quietly in the far corner, keeping his distance from the rest of the team.

"What's the matter, Brian? You're not worried about the leak, are you? I know it wasn't you…"

"No boss, it's not that. Can I have a quick word… somewhere more private?" he said, looking round the busy office.

Claire instinctively knew that something serious had happened. Brian was never like this… never this low. She followed him into an empty interview room and sat down in the seat next to him.

Brian didn't waste any time and got straight to the point. "It's Agnes ... she's got cancer!"

Claire's stomach dropped. "Oh God, how bad?"

"It's bad. Stage Four. She's to get a double mastectomy and then a course of chemotherapy."

"Oh Brian, I'm so sorry. Are you okay? Are you sure you should be here? Should you not be home with Agnes?" asked Claire.

"I wanted to, but Agnes insisted. She almost pushed me out the door this morning."

"She's a strong woman. How's she holding up?"

"Oh, you know Agnes, never one to wallow in bad news. She seems fine but... well, I think she's just putting on a brave face for my sake. Anyway, she was probably right to make me come to work. Take my mind off it for a bit."

Claire nodded in silence.

"So, what did your professor say about the killer?" he asked.

Claire knew that the sudden change of direction was deliberate but if that was how Brian wanted to cope, then that was fine with her. "Oh, quite a lot and I'm sure DCI Carter will share it with all of you in the briefing but more importantly, he's convinced someone in here has leaked the story to the press and is out for blood."

"One of us? You're kidding!" said Brian, shaking his head in disgust.

"How else could they know about the murder weapons? None of our press releases mentioned it."

Brian stopped to think about it. "Yeah, you're right. Jesus! What a mess! So, what's going to happen now?"

"Carter says he's going to get Woody to interview everyone and see who breaks but he's in with Milligan right now so who knows where that conversation will lead."

"Great! That's all we need in the middle of a bloody murder investigation. Come on, we'd better get back in there."

~

Carter's face was bright red when he entered the incident room, having just faced the wrath of his superior officer. He stood next to the incident board and addressed the room. "Right, you lot. Listen up. There's been a leak and Woody will be speaking to you all to find out which one of you useless bastards has been speaking to the press. But, before this happens, Detective Superintendent Milligan, has asked me to give whoever did this one chance to confess and save us all a lot of time. Own up now and the consequences will be less severe."

There was a silence in the room and all heads turned to see if anyone was brave enough to admit to their sins. To everyone's surprise, a single hand was raised.

"DC Doyle. I might have fuckin' known!" exclaimed Carter.

"But I didn't speak to the press, boss, honest." He hesitated before continuing. "But, I might have shared some information when speaking to the British Transport Police … about the hammer!"

Claire almost felt sorry for the young DC.

"Right," said Carter. "Well, well done for being brave enough to confess, son. I'll speak to you later… in private. Okay, now we have that sorted out, let's move on. DI Redding and I spoke to our profiler this morning and we have a few things to share."

Carter quickly summarised what Professor Tannock had said and then began allocating tasks to the team. He finished by asking Rambo to check Sheila Maxwell's mobile telephone, looking for anything suspicious or unusual: calls, texts, tweets, anything! He closed by reminding the team that they needed a quick result because, according to the Professor, it was only a matter of time before the next body would turn up.

Chapter 21

When Carter finished updating the team, he asked Doyle to see him outside. After a few minutes, Carter returned and informed the team that Doyle was now off the case and had been reassigned to support Dumbarton CID.

Claire was relieved that Carter had not gone overboard and suspended Doyle; he was young and would learn from his mistake. And to be fair, Doyle didn't actually share anything with the press; nevertheless, it was clear that Carter had to take some form of action to appease Milligan. Now that the drama was over, Claire decided to spend the rest of the day sifting through all the statements taken from the door-to-door interviews and getting up to speed with the two other murder files. It was clear from statements taken from local residents that the broken street lamp had only been smashed within the past few days. Coincidence? Perhaps, but Claire didn't believe in coincidence. She also noted that the search team had not found the missing facemask, so the killer may have been taking souvenirs. This prompted her to check the file on the second murder victim – Jackie Ross. The photographs and description of the murder scene were just as upsetting as the one in Craigendoran. Claire read the SOCO notes on the scene:

> *Four Fifteen a.m.*
> *Conditions – wet, moderate rainfall.*
> *Location - Knightsbridge Street, Glasgow, street poorly lit. Body hidden in wooded area bushes. Evidence that body had been dragged from kerb (likely location of first blow to head given the blood spatter pattern on the ground.)*
> *Victim - Appears to be middle-aged woman, shoulder-length blond hair. Massive head injury, severe loss of blood. Evidence of further blows to head while victim on ground. Victim wearing fawn-coloured winter coat (wool), black skirt, black tights (ripped), black high heels (left shoe - broken heel).*

Claire paused to consider what she had just read. *So, no facemask mentioned.* She took a mental note to cross reference this with the evidence lists held by Woody. *Was the victim wearing a facemask on the train?* She would need to check the witness statements. She read on. The SOCO noted that there were footprints at the scene due to the soft ground near the bushes. Plaster of Paris moulds of the imprints had been taken which had been later analysed and confirmed to be a UK, Size 13, training shoe. This gave an indication that the owner of the training shoes was at least six feet tall. *That fits the description given by McColl in terms of the height of their suspect and the image of the man caught on CCTV at Craigendoran station,* she thought. "Woody! Do we have the enhanced image of our suspect yet?"

Woody was standing marking up the incident board. "Yes, ma..., eh, Claire. I sent it to DCI Carter but it wasn't any good - he was wearing a facemask and it was dark, so enlarging the image only made it worse."

Claire was disappointed but not surprised. "Okay, thanks Woody. Oh, do you have the evidence list from the second murder – the one in Glasgow? I want to see if a facemask was listed."

"Yes, hold on." Woody stopped what he was doing and went over to the folders on the shelf, next to the window. He quickly found the correct folder and looked at the list. "Nope, no mention of a facemask. Why? Is it important?"

"Could be. Sheila Maxwell had a facemask and it appears to have vanished."

"A souvenir?" Woody offered.

"Yip. It's a possibility but I need to establish if the second victim had one to begin with."

"Ah," said Woody, "Hold on a minute. I saw mention of… yes, here it is. She was wearing an exemption tabard. You know, for folk who can't wear masks due to asthma or something, so she didn't have a facemask."

Claire's face said it all. "And another lead bites the dust."

Chapter 22

It had been a long and unproductive day for Claire. She had finished reviewing all the murder files and was no nearer to identifying the killer. The team had been busy tracking down all possible leads and the initial excitement of the CCTV footage and getting sight of the killer had slowly waned throughout the day as the investigation gradually ground to a halt. Carter and Milligan had spent most of the day dealing with the media and both men were ill-tempered and unapproachable. Accordingly, Claire decided to wait until the morning to ask Carter if she could visit the families of the first two victims: Grace Anderson and Jackie Ross. *Hopefully, he'll be in a better mood!*

As she made her way home, Claire thought about the positive way in which the day had started. Professor Tannock had certainly given her plenty to think about and she was pleased that the Professor had not completely ruled out her thoughts on there being a personal connection to the killings. Claire's gut feelings on such matters were almost always dependable, although she had to admit that she had been wrong about Baird – *what was his alibi again?* She made a mental note to look at the DCI's interview notes.

Her thoughts moved on and she started to replay her conversation with Brian over and over again. He had asked her to keep the news about Agnes to herself, which she would, but she would need to tell the DCI at some point. Brian didn't want to be taken off the case – like that poor sod, Doyle – and Claire didn't want Brian taken off the team either, so she was more than happy to respect his privacy, for now. However, she would need to tell Peter, who was struggling a bit himself at the moment. She wondered if he was having second thoughts about giving up work to watch the baby, now that she was pregnant. She hoped not. After all, the whole thing had been his idea. She would return to work as soon as physically possible and he would stay at home to look after their child. He didn't even seem that bothered about the financial impact that his loss of salary would inevitably have on the couple's standard of living – apparently, he had made a lot of money trading stock and didn't even have a mortgage to pay. They were lucky to be in that position and Claire had been stunned when Peter told her about his plan. But his initial enthusiasm seemed to have changed ever since she had told him about the pregnancy. Her gut was telling her that something just wasn't right and she was determined to get to the bottom of it.

~

Claire arrived home just after 6 p.m. and as soon as she opened the outside door, she could tell from the wonderful smells emanating from the kitchen that Peter had started to prepare their evening meal. "Hello, what's for tea?" she asked, popping her head through the kitchen door.

Sally immediately ran towards Claire to greet her, her tail wagging furiously with excitement.

"Pink pasta," said Peter. "It'll be ready in about ten minutes."

Claire loved Peter's pink pasta which was now a firm favourite of theirs.

"Perfect," said Claire, who then went upstairs to get changed.

When she returned to the kitchen, Peter was busy setting the small round table in the corner of the room.

"How was your day?" she asked.

"Oh, just the same old buying and selling shares, making money for strangers and the firm. Pretty uneventful really. How about you?"

Claire started to regale Peter with the highlights of her day, ending in the disappointment of her being no further closer to catching the killer.

"So, what do you do now?" he asked, genuinely interested in how the police dealt with a murder inquiry.

"Well, I hope to persuade DCI Carter to let me interview the families of the first two victims."

Peter screwed up his face in horror. "Oh, that doesn't sound like fun."

Claire shook her head. "It's not and I'll likely need to ask a few questions they've already answered more than once, so they may not welcome my visit."

"Rather you than me," said Peter. He didn't know why anyone would want to be a police officer. It was a thankless task, not to mention - dangerous. *Extremely dangerous!*

Claire could see Peter's mood drop a little and decided now was the time to push him a little further in the hope that he would finally open up to her and share how he was really feeling about the pregnancy. "Peter, I know something is bothering you. You've not been yourself for some time now. Is it the baby? Have you changed your mind about giving up your job?"

"No, it's not that... it's..." He held himself back from revealing the truth.

"Oh, come on Peter, there's no point trying to hide anything. Ever since I told you I was pregnant, you've changed. Can you blame me for thinking that your change of mood and the fact that I'm pregnant are not related?"

"No, but it's not that. Honest, it's…" He didn't have the heart to tell her.

"Well, if it's not that, what is it? What has caused you to be so upset?" Claire stopped herself. She suddenly remembered about Agnes and realised she hadn't told Peter. "I'm sorry, Peter, perhaps now is not the right time."

She walked over to him, put her arms around his waist and pulled him closer to her to hug him.

Peter hugged her back and then looked down to make eye contact. "What's the matter, Claire?"

"I'm afraid I've got some really sad news. It's Agnes… she's been diagnosed with cancer and it's not good. It's stage four."

Peter's initial relief that Claire had stopped asking about his mood turned to shock. "Stage four? But… how did they not pick it up sooner?" Claire had already processed the question and the answer was fairly obvious. "Screening was suspended during the pandemic or they might have caught it earlier."

"Oh God, poor Agnes and what about Brian? How's he taking it?"

"Not good. He's still at work, it's the best place for him, but I'm not sure how he'll be if things go pear-shaped."

"Has she? I mean, is she getting any treatment? It's not terminal, is it?" asked Peter.

"Oh, sorry, yes, she's to get a full mastectomy and chemotherapy but even then, the prognosis is not great."

The distressing news about Agnes made Peter realise that perhaps his problems were not that big a deal. He made up his mind there and then. He had put it off long enough. "Claire, there is something I need to tell you. Do you remember the morning that you told me that you were pregnant and I was on a call from a timeshare sales rep?" He paused to take a deep breath before continuing. "Well, it wasn't a sales call. It was someone making a threat."

Claire's face went pale. "What do you mean – making a threat?"

"He, the man on the line, said that if you testified, he would kill you and everyone that you loved." He stopped speaking to allow Claire to react to the news. He felt ashamed that he hadn't had the courage to mention it before now. However, her reaction was not quite what he was expecting - he thought she would go crazy, after all, he had withheld the truth from Claire and now she knew it.

"Did he mention Petrie by name?" she asked.

Peter suddenly realised that he was now dealing with DI Redding and not Claire MacDonald.

"No, I don't think he did. I just assumed it was Petrie or someone who worked for him."

Claire nodded. "Yes, too clever to mention his name but there's no doubt as to what was meant." She smiled at her hapless husband. She could now see the full picture. Peter's reaction to her news. His sudden change in mood. It all made sense – he was worried sick about her being hurt or worse. And Peter, being Peter, had kept it to himself all this time – all the worry and anxiety, which appeared every time she mentioned Petrie, burning inside him. It made perfect sense. "Peter, you are a silly dumpling. You know that, don't you?"

"A what?" Peter had been called many things in his life but he had never been called a 'silly dumpling' before, but he would take it. He thought Claire would be mad at him but she was the opposite; she was... relieved. "So, you're not angry?"

"Well, I should be, shouldn't I?" she said sharply, and then her left cheek rose slowly into a smirk and then formed a cheeky grin. "Of course, not. I get it, Peter. I understand why you didn't want to tell me at first and couldn't tell me later. You really are a daft sausage."

He nodded and smiled. For the first time in weeks, he could breathe easily again. A huge weight had been lifted off his shoulders.

"I suppose I'll need to report the threat to HQ," she said nonchalantly.

Peter's face turned pale. "What? Will I need to give a statement?"

"No, I don't think so. It would have been different if Petrie were still alive but now that the threat has gone…"

"But what about the other guy? The one awaiting trial?"

"Oh, you mean, Bull. Yes, there will be a trial for him but he's just a small cog in the wheel. Nobody is going to go to the trouble of killing a police officer over someone like him. He might even change his plea to guilty to get a reduced sentence. It happens all the time."

"You're kidding?"

"Nope. George Chapman certainly knew what he was talking about - the law is an ass."

"George who?"

Claire smiled at Peter. "He was an English writer in the 17th cent…" She could see Peter's eyes glaze over. "Never mind, it's not important."

~

The assassin had received his instructions and was making his way to Dumbarton by car. He had booked a room in the Abbotsford Hotel and was looking forward to a hearty meal, a few drinks and a good night's sleep before getting to work. He planned to follow the detective for a few days, learning as much as he could about her movements until he was confident that it would be safe to kill her. The job had been made more difficult by the request that it should look like an accident. This didn't surprise him, given that the target was a police officer. He knew that it would not be easy and that he would need to be patient and most of all, careful.

Chapter 23

The team met at 8.00 a.m. sharp to hear the morning briefing by DCI Carter. His mood was considerably better than it had been the previous day and he appeared to have forgotten all about the media leak and was now fully focussed on catching the killer.

Claire waited for Carter to finish the briefing before approaching him. "Sir, can I have a word?"

"Sure, what's up?"

"I was thinking of going through to Coatbridge to speak to Grace Anderson's family and take a look at the scene of the crime. You know, get a better feel for it, rather than just relying on what's in the file."

If Carter was unhappy with the request, he didn't show it. "Still think you will find something that we missed?"

"No, it's not that. It's just I don't feel connected to those murders – not being involved in the initial investigation. And now that we know we are after a serial killer, it would be good optics if someone spoke to the families and provided an update on where we are with the case."

Carter hadn't thought about the latter point. "Actually, that's not a bad idea Claire. Do you want me to come along and introduce you?"

"No, you've got your work cut out here, and the Super will want his daily update, but I can take Brian with me if that's okay. The pregnant worker risk assessment indicated I shouldn't go out on my own."

"Sorry, you're... you're pregnant?" Carter was visibly surprised.

"Yes, sir. I assumed DCI Mitchell would have told you when she agreed to release me."

Carter shook his head. "Well, I suppose it doesn't really matter now."

Claire stood there waiting for his decision. "So, I can go and take Brian with me?"

"Yes, I suppose so," he conceded. "I'll get Woody to phone ahead and let the family know that you are coming."

"Thank you, sir." Claire turned and made a beeline for Brian.

"Brian, grab your jacket. We're heading to Coatbridge."

Chapter 24

The car journey to Coatbridge was uneventful; the M8 and A89 were quiet and the two detectives arrived at Coatdyke station within forty-five minutes. Claire had decided that she wanted to walk the route from the station to the crime scene to get a feel for the area and to try and get into the killer's mind, and after that, they would visit Mr Anderson, who was at home having completed a night shift at the hospital. He was annoyed that Woody had woken him up but had agreed to speak to DI Redding and DS O'Neill.

Brian parked the unmarked car in the station car park and the two detectives made their way to the ramp, which they surmised Grace Anderson would have used to exit the station. They walked quickly towards Dumbeth Park, entered via the gated entrance and proceeded towards where the body had been found. There were still some traces of the blue police tape tied to some trees but given it had been over a year since the murder had taken place, the site was no longer off limits to the public.

"Well, this is the spot," said Brian, pointing to the torn tape.

Claire carefully stepped onto the grass and had a quick look at the area behind the bushes. "According to the blood spatter analysis, she was struck by the hammer on the pavement and then was dragged behind the rhododendron bushes, where her head received further blows from the hammer. The hammer itself was found lying beside the body, just like with Sheila Maxwell."

Brian nodded and looked around. "It would be pretty dark here at night."

"Yes, it makes you wonder why she chose this route."

Brian was quick to respond. "Quickest way home - I had a look on Google Maps. It would take her another five minutes to get home if she went around the park."

"Yeah, it's interesting though - looking at the case file differently, now that we know we're after a serial killer. The initial investigation was based on the assumption that the killer was waiting for his victim – the focus was on someone who knew her.

The husband was interviewed on four separate occasions. Poor sod!"

"Yes, and now we know that it wasn't him and suspect that the killer is choosing his victims randomly, having spotted them on the train," Brian added.

"Well, I'm not so sure that he is picking out the victims randomly. After all, they were all middle-aged, attractive blondes."

"So, you still think it could be personal?" asked Brian.

"Not just me. Professor Tannock didn't rule it out either. What I can't understand is why the gaps between these killings. I mean, this one was when - 15th November 2019? Then the one in Glasgow was a few months later and then a large gap between that one and the last one. Doesn't make any sense. Does it?"

"Well, we are looking for a psychopath. I suppose it wouldn't make any sense to us, but it might to him."

"Yeah, if we only knew what was going through his twisted head - it might give us a clue as to who we're looking for." Claire took a final look around. "Well, I think I've seen enough. Let's go speak to Mr Anderson."

"I've got to be honest, boss. I'm not looking forward to this at all. The poor man has lost his wife. It's been over a year, the killer hasn't been found and suddenly we turn up, asking him the same questions over again, making him relive the nightmare."

"I know Brian. It's not fair, but we have a job to do. Come on, let's get back to the car. The quicker we get there, the quicker it will be over."

Chapter 25

It only took the two detectives a few minutes to drive the short distance from the station to Eglington Drive, home of Barry Anderson. Claire rang the doorbell of the modest terraced house and stood back. The door was opened by a man, whom Claire assumed was Barry Anderson. He looked tired and was unshaven, wearing loose jogging bottoms and a t-shirt.

"Mr Anderson?"

"Yes," he growled.

"I'm DI Claire Redding and this is DS Brian…"

"Aye, okay. I know who you are. The station called me and warned me you were coming. Right, you'd better come in then."

They followed Anderson into the front room, which smelled bad and looked worse. Anderson noticed DI Redding's reluctance to sit down and immediately started to remove debris from the couch. "Sorry, about the mess. Ever since Grace died … Well, there doesn't seem much point in keeping the place tidy. It's just me now."

"What about your son?" Claire asked tentatively. "Does he still live here?"

"Nah, he's got digs near his university. It's understandable. Too many memories of his mum around here and I… Well, I've not been at my best, since Grace passed."

"I'm really sorry to hear that, Mr Anderson," said Claire, taking a seat on the couch. Brian did the same.

"So, DI Redding, what is it you want to speak to me about?"

"I suppose you'll have seen the news reports that we are now looking for a serial killer, who we now believe is responsible for the murder of your wife and two other women."

"Aye, I saw it. Do you know that the local police thought it was me at first? Bloody useless lot of pricks," he hissed.

"Yes, I've read the case file. But now that we believe that we are looking for a serial killer, we are investigating the three murders in a completely different light."

"I bet you are. So, who are you, exactly?"

"Sorry, I should have explained. We are from Dumbarton CID but have been attached to the Major Incident Team to assist with the investigation. The third murder took place in Craigendoran, which is on my patch. So, I have been going over all three murders, trying to find something which links the three killings and…"

"And have you? Found anything?" he asked.

"Not yet. Is it okay if I ask you a few questions about Grace?"

"Sure. Fire away, hen."

Claire cringed at the 'hen' reference. It was a personal hate of hers, but in the interest of keeping Anderson onside she ignored it and moved on.

"Thank you. We now believe the killer targets his victims on the train and follows them before attacking. Did Grace use the train regularly?"

"Yeah, every day, well every mid-weekday, she worked in Glasgow," he explained.

"Right, and what time did she normally travel?"

"First thing in the morning – about 8 a.m., and then coming home about 5.30 p.m. to 6 p.m."

"I see, but on the night of her death, she was later. Was that planned?"

"No. She stayed on late to have some drinks with work colleagues. She had an interview that day and was promoted."

"Right, so it would have been a pure coincidence that she happened to be on that train at that time."

"Yes, I suppose so. But why is that relevant?" he asked.

"I'm trying to establish if the killer had been stalking your wife prior to her murder or whether it was completely random."

"I see," said Anderson. "So, it looks like it was random then."

"Yes, it looks that way," said Claire. "Can I also ask? The route your wife took home that night - was it normal for her to take a shortcut through the park?"

"Yes, but I had warned her about it. It can be pretty dark, especially in the winter."

"Yes, we had a look before we got here. Street lighting was poor - the perfect spot to get away with murder." Claire regretted saying it as soon as the words left her mouth. If her remarks had upset Anderson, he showed no sign of it.

"The local police were working on the theory that the killer hid behind the bushes and then sprung out and attacked Grace from behind. Do you still think that's what happened?" asked Anderson.

"Well, not based on what we believe happened in Craigendoran. We're convinced the killer followed his victims off the train and then picked a poorly lit spot to attack them," said Claire.

"How do you know that? Have you got a witness or CCTV footage? You must have something to go on which makes you think that."

Claire looked nervously at Brian, whose eyes were giving a clear signal to say nothing.

Anderson read the eye contact between the two officers. "You do have something don't you? What is it? A witness or CCTV?" he asked.

Claire felt she had to offer him something and chose her words very carefully. "There is some CCTV footage of a man we suspect may have followed Sheila Maxwell, the woman who was killed in Craigendoran, but we couldn't identify him as the image quality was poor and he was wearing a facemask."

"But you do think it was him. The man who was caught on CCTV."

"Yes, we do, but as I said we have no idea who he is. He was wearing a COVID facemask. We just have a basic description…" Claire stopped speaking as it suddenly occurred to her that Grace had been killed prior to the COVID pandemic and therefore if the killer had been caught on CCTV at Coatdyke, they might have a chance of seeing his face. The question was - did the original investigation team in Coatbridge get a copy of the CCTV? Probably not, if they were working on the theory that the killer was local and was hiding in the bushes.

Anderson broke her line of thought. "What did he look like?"

"Sorry?" she asked.

"This man on the CCTV, do you have a description?"

"Sorry, I can't share that with you, Mr Anderson. In fact, I've said too much already."

"Oh, come on, Detective. Don't you think I deserve to know?"

"I'm sorry, Mr Anderson. Really, I am, but the description has only been shared among the police community. We don't want to raise public alarm and we don't want vigilantes running around attacking every man who matches the description of our suspect. Also, we don't want our suspect to know we're looking for him, but believe me – we are. The British Transport Police have been put on alert and will report any sighting of anyone who matches the description."

"I suppose that makes sense," he conceded. "Will you let me know if you catch him? It's burning me up knowing that the bastard is still out there. I want to see him … I … I want to see the bastard's face when you lock him up and throw away the key."

"You can count on it, Mr Anderson," said Claire, standing up to leave. "Thank you for your time."

"Oh, one last thing Inspector. When will I get Grace's possessions back?"

"Oh, I'm sorry but if you are referring to what she was wearing when she was killed then we need to keep that as evidence until we catch the killer and go to trial."

Anderson looked dismayed. "I'm not bothered about what she was wearing, Detective. It's her personal items. You know – her wedding rings, necklace, and earrings. That sort of stuff.

Claire nodded sympathetically. "I'm sorry, everything she had on her person at the time of death is considered evidence, but you will get it back... eventually."

Claire could tell that Anderson was less than convinced with her response.

~

The two officers made their way back to the car, each deep in thought and unaware that they were being watched.

"Poor sod," said Brian as he shuffled into the driving seat.

"Yeah," agreed Claire. "Brian, when we get back to the station, can you check with Coatbridge CID to see if they have any CCTV footage from the cameras at Coatdyke station. I know they weren't looking in that direction back then, but you never know. Someone with a bit of savvy might have thought about checking it and have a copy somewhere. I don't think there was any reference to it in the case file, but you never know."

"It's certainly worth checking, boss. Right, so where to next?"

Chapter 26

Claire had decided to visit the scene of the second murder in Anniesland and accordingly, the car left the M8, joining the part of the A82 known as Great Western Road and heading for Anniesland Cross. According to the case file, Jackie Ross was heading back to her mother's house from Anniesland station when she had been attacked. Claire had asked Woody to let Jackie's mother know that they would pay her a visit but he had been unable to contact her at home and had no other means of getting in touch – there was no mobile phone number listed on the file. Nevertheless, Claire decided that it would still be useful to see the crime scene for themselves since it was more or less on the way back to Dumbarton.

Brian parked the car in the station car park. Both officers got out and headed to the station to get a look at the position of the CCTV cameras and to work out the likely route that Jackie would have used to walk to her mother's house on Knightsbridge Street. Having taken photographs of the station layout and exits on both sides of the track, they made their way back to Great Western Road and crossed over the busy road using the nearest set of traffic lights. They followed the quickest route to the house using Google Maps. It was no surprise to Claire that the killer had waited until Jackie had almost made it to her mother's house before attacking and dragging her into a small, wooded area just off Knightsbridge Street. It would have been too risky to try this anywhere else along the route.

When they arrived at the scene of the crime, Claire could see that the blue tape was more intact than it had been in Coatdyke – an early indication that the crime was more recent. "Well, what do you think, Brian?"

Brian looked around at the trees and the obvious gaps between them and the road. "He took a bit of a chance doing it here." He turned and faced back to the road. "Only 5 metres to the road – he could easily have been seen by a passer-by, albeit it was late at night."

"Yip, and yet he didn't. Well, he must have been determined to kill someone on that particular night to take such a chance."

Brian nodded. "Or desperate! Remember, Jackie Ross was on the last train home from a night out with friends in Glasgow so this would have been his last chance to make a kill."

"Good point, Brian. Hold on, if that was the last train, how did he get home?"

"Depends on where he lives, I suppose. He could have caught a taxi or walked home, if he lives close enough."

"Good point," Claire responded. "We should contact the local taxi companies - everything they do these days is recorded on their systems. We have an approximate time and a rough idea of the location where he might have called or hailed down a black cab, so yes, why not. I'll get someone else from the team to check that when we get back. Come on Brian, the game is afoot!"

"What?"

Claire giggled to herself. "Never mind. It's not important."

~

The assassin had followed the unmarked car all the way to Coatdyke, then to Anniesland and back to Police HQ in Dumbarton. He hadn't learned much about her movements, as clearly she was out and about investigating some case or another, but now that she was back in Dumbarton, he hoped to learn more about her behaviour and habits and find a weak spot. So far, she had not gone out on her own so it was unlikely that the opportunity would arise during the working day but he would be patient and observe her movements. He had all the time in the world!

Chapter 27

When Claire and Brian finally made it back to the incident room, the telephones were ringing off the hook. Apparently, every Tom, Dick and Harry had been calling in to say they thought they knew the serial killer. However, none had any evidence to back up their suspicions and were quickly dismissed from the investigation.

Claire looked around the room, "Woody, where's Carter?"

"He's in with Milligan and ACC Blackford."

"The Assistant Chief Constable is here?"

"Yeah, and she's not very happy."

"Right. Well, I can guess why; all this media attention we're now getting and the increased public fear and anxiety. Anyway, I can see you're all busy. Is there anything I should know about?"

"Nope, it's a bloody circus in here. We really need to get this guy soon. What about you, anything?"

"Not really. Brian will see if the Coatbridge CID have any CCTV from the Grace Anderson murder investigation."

"They better not have. We asked them for everything when we took over the case."

"True, but given they weren't looking in that direction I just wondered if someone had taken the initiative and got the CCTV, albeit it didn't feature heavily as part of their investigation." Claire was being generous.

Woody grunted. "There will be hell to pay if that's the case. Anything else?"

"Yes, I would like someone to check with all the taxi companies that operate in the Anniesland area. I'm looking for a note of all the hires that were taken in that area around midnight on the night of the Jackie Ross murder. I want to know how the killer got home that night. We believe Jackie was on the last train, so did he take a taxi or was he within walking distance? Either way, we might learn something."

"Christ almighty! Why didn't we think of that?"

"Don't know. You'll need to speak to the DCI about it."

"Aye, that'll be right. Okay, I'll give it to Patsy to check out. The other two are needed here to handle the calls."

"Thanks Woody. Oh, and now that I've spoken with Grace Anderson's husband, could I take another look at the evidence list? He was asking about getting her jewellery back. Obviously he'll need to wait, but I want to check what we're holding."

"Sure. I'll bring it over to your desk." He turned and made his way over to the folders on the shelf.

Claire sat down at her desk. Brian, who was sitting at the desk next to hers, was speaking to someone in Coatbridge CID about the CCTV. It didn't sound too hopeful.

"Here you go," said Woody, handing the evidence list to Claire.

"Thanks Woody." Claire quickly reviewed the list and immediately something jumped out at her. There was only one ring listed. The wedding band was missing! She was sure Anderson had said rings. "Woody, sorry to be a pest but can you get me the SOCO photos taken at the scene of the Grace Anderson murder? I want to see any photos of her hands."

Woody, who had started to give instructions to Patsy, turned back towards Claire. "Why, what are you looking for?"

"I'm pretty sure Barry Anderson told me she was wearing wedding rings but the inventory only lists the engagement ring," she explained.

Woody looked perturbed. "Are you sure? I doubt the SOCO would have made that type of mistake."

Claire turned towards Brian who had just finished his call to Coatbridge. "Brian, do you remember Barry Anderson mentioning wedding rings – plural, when he asked about getting Grace's possessions back?"

"Yeah, he definitely said rings."

Woody turned and went back to the folder to retrieve the SOCO photographs. "Here they are," he said. He looked through them to find shots of the victim's hands. "Yes, got them." He looked closely at the enlarged image of the left hand – now that he knew what he was looking for, it was very obvious. There was a thin white band of skin immediately above the engagement ring. The wedding ring had been removed. "Shit, I can't believe we missed that," said Woody, turning back towards Claire and Brian.

"Missed what?" hissed Carter, who had just returned to the room.

Woody hesitated and Claire took the initiative to fill the awkward silence. "We now know that the killer is taking souvenirs, sir. As you know, we have a missing facemask and now there is a missing wedding band - taken from Grace Anderson."

"What the fuck!" Carter exclaimed. "How did the SOCO miss that?"

Woody said nothing and handed the photograph to the DCI who quickly scanned the photo and came to the same conclusion as the others. "Jesus Christ, almighty! So, what about the second victim? Do we have any idea what he might have taken?"

Woody shook his head. "I've no idea."

Claire was a step ahead of the DCI and was already going over what she had read in the case file earlier that day. "Wait a minute. Woody, the SOCO report on Jackie Ross, I think it might have mentioned a shoe with a broken heel."

Woody didn't need to be asked. He went and retrieved the case file and quickly found the evidence list. "Yes, both shoes are listed, one with a broken heel."

"Yes," said Claire, "But where is the missing heel? Is that listed?"

Woody scanned the file. "No mention of it."

"For fuck's sake!" said Carter. "What else have we missed?" He wasn't expecting an answer.

Claire thought twice about adding fuel to the fire but knew he would need to know at some point. "Well sir, DS O'Neill and I were wondering how the killer made his way home…"

Carter didn't let her finish the sentence. "I know Detective, from Craigendoran station, without the cameras picking him up. We've already highlighted that as…"

"No sir, we were wondering how the killer made his way home from Anniesland if Jackie Ross was on the last train."

Carter went cold. He couldn't blame the SOCO for that one. "Jee...sus Christ! How did I miss that? I should have…"

"Let's not dwell on that now, sir," said Claire, making light of the oversight. "Woody has asked Patsy to check with all local taxi companies to see if there were any hires taken in the area around the time of the murder. Although, as DS O'Neill suggested, he might live close enough to walk home."

"Either way we learn something," said Carter.

"Yes, sir," said Claire, smiling to herself.

"Dare I ask if you two discovered anything else on your travels?" asked Carter.

"Well sir, we did think of asking Coatbridge CID to provide CCTV footage from Coatdyke station at the time of the Grace Anderson murder," said Claire coyly, anticipating the inevitable explosion.

"What fucking CCTV footage? There had better not be any fucking footage. There was no mention of it in the case file."

It was Brian's turn to be brave and share his knowledge. "I've just checked with the DI in charge over there, Brian Davidson, and he says that they did take a quick look at the CCTV footage in order to establish that Grace Anderson was on that particular train but that was all."

Carter's face could not get any redder. "So, they didn't bother to share that with us or mention it in the case file?"

Brian took a deep breath. "Well, the thing is, sir, the DI is adamant that it was referred to somewhere in the case file."

"Where? I haven't seen it. Woody, have you seen anything?" asked Carter.

"Did this… DI Davidson, did he give you any indication where it was mentioned in the files?"

"Yes, he said it was referred to in his handover notes on the case."

"Well, I've not seen them! Woody - check the file carefully, see if you can find the missing notes."

"Yes, sir." Woody walked away with the case file under his arm, relieved that he was out of the firing line for now.

"So, Brian, what about this CCTV footage? Do they still have it?" asked Carter.

"He's not sure, sir. He's looking for it now."

"Right then. Well, he better find it, or there will be hell to pay."

Chapter 28

The killer sat at home, eyes glued to the television, scanning the news for any sign that the police might be onto him. There had been a lot of local media coverage about the killings in the last few days, and even the odd report on the national news channels, but it seemed to have settled down a little now, especially as the police were unable to offer any real hope of catching the killer and were still pleading for any witnesses to come forward. He knew they must have a decent description of him by now and maybe even some images from the CCTV, so he considered changing his appearance again.

He was delighted that his ruse had managed to fool the police so far and sat there contemplating if he should strike again and how soon. He had surprised himself at how good it made him feel, but the euphoric release of anger didn't last, and he soon had felt a craving for another murder. This had never been his intention; he had been focussed on releasing his anger in the most brutal way possible and had succeeded, but now that he had successfully killed three people, he hungered for more.

He weighed up the risks of being caught, especially now that everyone and their granny was looking for him. Perhaps, it was too soon. He would need to wait at least another month to avoid suspicion, but he knew that with each passing day, the urge to kill would return. He decided that he had to wait until all the media attention settled down and then carefully select another target. Perhaps he would change his methodology a little to confuse the police. *Yes, that would be fun!*

Chapter 29

Claire made her way home, feeling much better about the progress that she and Brian had made on the case that day. She was also pleased that they were able to have a good heart-to-heart about Agnes in the car on the way to Coatdyke. She had offered him her personal support if things got rough with Agnes and had also mentioned the various well-being supports which the police offered by way of counselling, etc. As expected, Brian had shrugged off any offer of help but thanked Claire for honouring her promise to keep news of Agnes private and had promised to let her know if he did need anything. Knowing Brian, that was very unlikely.

As she walked the short distance to her home on Silverton Avenue, Claire was completely unaware that she was being followed. He already knew where she lived and was careful to keep a good distance between himself and her to avoid any risk of detection.

Claire made her way down to Crosslet Road and from there headed along the cycle path to Silverton Avenue. It was only as she approached the small bridge over the burn that she remembered Peter had texted her to ask her to pick up milk on the way home. So instead of turning right to cross the bridge, she turned left and cut through Silvertonhill Lane to connect to Crosslet Road and then up onto Alclutha Avenue, where the small post office and grocery shop was situated.

He decided to follow her to see where she was going. *Why the sudden change of direction? Had she spotted him? Was she waiting to confront him around the next corner?* He decided to proceed with even more caution than before and allowed even more distance to form between them. He turned onto Alclutha Avenue, spotted her striding towards Greenhead Road, and decided to follow her along the quiet tree-lined street. *Where was she going?*

Claire turned into the Silverton Post Office, bought a carton of semi-skimmed milk, headed straight back out the door and turned back the way she came. He was waiting outside the shop, pretending to be looking at his phone when she reappeared. He decided to let her pass him and wait before following her again. He kept his eyes on his phone avoiding any eye contact with her.

As she got closer, Claire saw the man standing looking at his phone and moved onto the other side of the pavement to pass him, which she did without incident. He waited until she was a good distance away and then followed her all the way home.

When Claire arrived home, she immediately noticed that there were no smells coming from the kitchen. *Unusual.* She made her way into the kitchen to put the milk into the fridge and found Peter, sitting at the table. "Hello. Everything okay?" she asked.

"Yes, do you fancy going out for a meal tonight? I hear there's a new place opened in Helensburgh which is supposed to be nice."

"You're clearly in a better mood."

"Yes, I know. Sorry, I've not been myself since that phone call but now the threat is over… well, you know what I mean."

"Yeah, why not?" said Claire. "It'll be nice to get out again. Can I drive your car?"

Claire loved Peter's BMW, but he was very precious about letting her drive it.

"Tell you what. I'll drive us there and you can drive back. That way I can have a glass of wine with the meal," he suggested.

"Fine by me," said Claire, smiling. "I'll just go upstairs and get changed."

~

He watched them leave the house and approach the Black BMW. He took note of the number plate and then decided to head back to his hotel for something to eat. He had left his hired car outside the station and had decided to leave it there overnight; he would follow her to work on foot the next morning. He had already noted that she started work at 8 a.m. and would be ready for her.

Chapter 30

Claire and Peter arrived at the restaurant in time to make their 7 p.m. booking. They put their facemasks on to enter the public place, as was still required by law. Peter then led the way and opened the outside door for Claire to enter first, but she had to quickly step aside as a man, also wearing a facemask, was just leaving. He brushed past Peter, looked briefly at Claire, and then hurriedly made his way onto the pavement. It was only when they were both inside the restaurant waiting to be seated that Claire thought that she recognised the man who had just passed them but couldn't place him. She let the thought drift as the waiter attended to them, confirmed their booking on the system and led them to their table.

"This looks nice," said Peter, looking around and taking in the atmosphere of the restaurant.

"Yes," agreed Claire. "Let's hope the food is just as good."

"Should be, it's getting lots of good reviews."

Claire lifted up the menu to see what was on offer. "Peter, have you seen the price of the starters'?" she asked, blowing air from her pouted lips and whistling.

"Yes, and it's fine, so order whatever you like and don't worry about the cost."

"If you say so." Her eyes moved up and down the menu, looking for the cheapest choices.

Peter made up his mind quickly and put his menu down to indicate that he was ready to order. "So, how was your day? Catch any bad guys?" His usual conversation opener where Claire was concerned.

"Nope, but we are making some progress."

"And you're convinced it's not the guy you arrested?"

"Firstly, I didn't arrest him. It was DCI Mitchell, and yes, I'm convinced he didn't do it. He had a solid alibi which has been checked."

"Right, but you still think it was personal?"

The conversation stopped briefly as the waiter approached their table and took the order. It gave Claire time to think of a response.

"Well, yes and no. That was my gut feeling but now I'm not so sure, although I really need to…" Claire stopped speaking suddenly as her mind changed direction.

Peter was left hanging. "What is it, Claire? What do you need to do?"

"What? Sorry. Yes, I meant to read over the transcript of his interview with DCI Mitchell but I've been too distracted with other matters. Do you mind if I put a note in my phone to check this tomorrow? I don't know if it's the pregnancy or something else that's affecting my memory, but I'm forgetting to do stuff."

"Sure. Go ahead, but you've lost me. If you know he has an alibi and it has been checked out, why are you even bothering?"

Claire had to concede that Peter had a point. "You're right, but it's just me being me. I don't know why but I just want to know. This investigation has been a bit weird for me and Brian. I mean - we've joined it late in the day and we're only really catching up with the other murders. Although you should have seen DCI Carter's face today - Brian and I took a closer look at the first two murder scenes and found a few things that they had missed, or to be fair, we found a few things which the initial investigation of these cases hadn't picked up on. Anyway, he was absolutely livid and the air was blue."

Peter smiled. He could only imagine the type of language used in a police station in the middle of such a high-profile case. What surprised him was how relaxed Claire seemed to be about it all. "So, how is Brian doing? Did you get a chance to speak to him, offer support, like we discussed?"

"Yeah, we had a good chat on the way up to Coatdyke."

"Coatdyke? As in Coatbridge?"

Claire had forgotten that Peter was a Lanarkshire boy. "Yes, the first murder took place in Dumbeth Park."

"You're kidding me on. I used to play football there when I was wee."

The conversation was interrupted again by the waiter, who had returned with their starters and drinks. Peter's eyes lit up at the sight of his favourite starter of all time – scallops. Claire had gone for the more conservative choice of homemade vegetable soup. Both agreed that their starters were delicious and quickly devoured them before continuing with the conversation.

"So, Dumbeth Park?" asked Peter, keen to find out more.

"Yes, although why she chose to make her way home via the park in the dark is beyond me," said Claire.

"Human nature, I suppose. Probably the shortest route."

"Yeah, she lived on the other side of the park. Only a few minutes away from where she was killed."

"Poor woman!" said Peter.

A waitress came and cleared the plates from the table.

"Yes, I met her husband today. Poor man, he was in such a mess."

"Yeah, just like I would be if anything happened to you … and the baby," said Peter, his face turning serious for the first time that evening.

Claire reached over and touched his hand affectionately and then withdrew as a waiter returned with their main courses, fillet steak for Peter and Caesar Salad for Claire.

"You don't need to worry about me, Peter. I can handle myself," she said softly.

Peter didn't want to spoil the night so he let the point drop. "Well, this looks good," he said, his eyes going between the two meals."

After a few bites, they both agreed that the restaurant would become a regular for them both; there were a few good restaurants in Helensburgh but this one was special. Of course, it was not as convenient as the Abbotsford Hotel, their local haunt; they both had a soft spot for it as it was where they had their first date. But it was more than that; the meals were good and its friendly owners were always keen to chat with hotel guests and make them feel welcome.

After finishing the main course, they both agreed that they were completely and utterly stuffed and could not eat another morsel. Peter paid the bill and they made their way to the exit.

Chapter 31

Claire's mobile phone rang on her bedside table at 5.45 a.m. She stretched her arm out, grabbed the phone and whispered, "Hello, DI Redding here."

"Good morning, ma'am, Sergeant Moody here. A body has been found in East End Park with a similar MO to the Craigendoran killing. Since you live near the park, DCI Carter has asked you to get there a.s.a.p. and secure the area. He'll get there as soon as he can. I've a couple of uniforms on site and more on their way."

Claire's heart started to race. *Another one – so soon!* "Right, I'm on my way," she said and quickly got out of bed. Peter groaned a little at being disturbed and rolled over to try and get back to sleep. He was used to Claire receiving calls in the middle of the night and learned not to ask any questions – it only made it more difficult for him to go back to sleep.

Claire dressed quickly and made her way out the front door as quietly as possible. She headed for the cycle path and jogged towards the park, which was only a couple of minutes away. As soon as the park came into view, she saw the flashing blue lights of the police car and then spotted the two uniformed officers. One officer had started to secure the area with tape while the other was speaking to a member of the public, who was struggling to control her dog, presumably the person who found the body. Claire made a beeline for the area where the body had been found, displayed her ID to the officer speaking to the woman with the dog, then cut across the grass and immediately felt her feet sink into the soft ground. She stopped herself, taking a wide berth around the body and approached it from the rear. Another police vehicle arrived via the Crosslet Road exit and parked on the path. The two police officers then made their way straight to the scene. Claire shouted to them to assist the officer with the tape, widen the cordon and keep the public well away from the scene. Confident that the crime scene was now secure, Claire examined the area around the body and noticed some heavy indents in the ground: boot prints. Claire also noticed that the heel of the right footprint looked deeper than the left one.

Claire put on a pair of latex gloves, which she always carried in her jacket pocket, and knelt down to examine the body. The victim looked to be in her early thirties and was dressed casually, without an overcoat. Her head had been smashed by a blunt instrument; a hammer was lying on the ground to the victim's left. However, it was obvious that it did not match the description of the hammer used in the first three murders. Claire carefully searched the body for identification and found none. She looked more closely at the woman's face and noticed that the blood on the side of her cheek had been smeared. Satisfied that she had seen all that she needed to see, Claire approached the officer and the woman with the dog – a large, cream-coloured Labrador.

"Hi, I'm DI Redding, and you are?"

"PC Dave Campbell. This is Irene Redpath. I have taken note of her details and…"

"Thanks, Dave. That's great. You can go and help the others guard the perimeter until the SOCO gets here."

"Yes, ma'am," he said, slightly miffed by her abruptness.

Claire turned to the young woman with the dog. "Hello, I believe you found the body?"

"Yes, I live just over there." She turned and pointed towards the row of houses which backed onto the cycle path. "I always let Maisie out before I head off to work. She usually runs around on the grass area to the front, does her business and then comes straight back in for her breakfast, but this morning she went over to the woods and wouldn't respond to my calls. She's normally very obedient, especially when tempted with the offer of food. I had to go over to get her and that's when I found Chrissie, lying there…"

"Sorry, you know the victim?"

"Yes, she's Chrissie Parker. She lives a few doors down from me." She turned and pointed to the victim's backdoor.

"And does she live there alone?" asked Claire.

"No, she lives with her boyfriend. Well, her partner – they're not married."

"What's his name?"

"Dan… sorry, I can't remember his surname."

"That's okay. So, how would you describe their relationship?"

"Oh, I wouldn't like to say, I don't really know them that well. You don't think he did it. I thought it was the serial killer - you know, with one with the hammer!"

"It's really too early to say," said Claire, keen not to give any information away. "Did you approach the body?"

"Well, only to pull Maisie back. I'm afraid she was licking Chrissie's face when I got there."

"Right," said Claire. *That explains the smeared blood.* "Okay, thank you. We'll need to take a full statement later if that's okay. Can I ask you to return home for now? And stay there until I can get someone over…"

"But, what about my work?" she pleaded.

"Sorry, but you'll need to let them know that you're needed here. To be honest, you really shouldn't go in - this must have been quite a shock."

"Yes, it was, but I'm a nurse so it's not the first dead body that I've seen."

Claire nodded but didn't quite think this was the same thing. "I see. Well, please tell your manager that the police has instructed you to stay at home today and if they need confirmation, give them my details." Claire removed a small business card from her inside jacket pocket and handed it to Ms Redpath.

Chapter 32

DCI Carter arrived at the scene just as the SOC team were setting up the tent. "Morning Claire. Well, is it number four?" he asked.

"Don't think so, sir," she responded.

"Right, so what do we have then?"

"Okay, so the murder weapon was a hammer, but as you can see, it's different from the type used in the other murders. Also, the victim was clearly in her early thirties, has dark brown shoulder-length hair and does not have a coat. It is therefore unlikely that she was targeted from a train journey unless the killer took the coat as a souvenir."

"Unlikely," responded Carter.

Claire continued, "According to the woman who found the body, the victim, Chrissie Parker, lives in that house over there, along with her partner, Dan something, surname unknown. I'm getting the electoral register checked to get the full name. We knocked on his door and rang the doorbell but had no response. I've also requested a warrant to allow us access and I'm just waiting for the duty Sergeant to call back with confirmation."

"Good work, Claire. I suppose there's not much more we can do here until the SOC team have done their work and the warrant arrives."

"I've got one or two of the uniforms speaking to the neighbours on either side of the victim's house to see if anyone heard anything unusual last night," Claire added.

"Good. Okay, if this is not *our* killer then I'm going to suggest that we hand it over to DCI Mitchell to investigate. We don't need this distraction interfering with our work."

"Yes, sir."

Claire spotted PC Campbell leave the house to the left of the victim's and could see that he was heading straight for the two detectives.

"What do you have for us, Constable... eh, Campbell, was it?" asked Claire.

"Yes ma'am, apparently the neighbour on the left of the victim's house heard some shouting around about midnight but then it went quiet, so they didn't bother reporting it."

"Right. That's good enough for me," said Carter. "Stuff the warrant. We're going in now. Constable - get a battering ram and a couple of other uniformed officers ready to assist."

The young officer turned on his heels and ran over to his colleagues who were standing beside the police vehicles. He retrieved the small red battering ram from the vehicle's boot and three of them headed to the backdoor of the property. Carter rattled the door and shouted, "Police, open up!" He was just about to give the order to break into the house when the upstairs window opened and a half-naked man leaned out and shouted. "What the fuck is going on?"

Carter looked up at the red-eyed man, who clearly had just woken up. "Police, open up or we'll break in."

"What? Hold on. I'm coming down."

Twenty seconds later, the backdoor opened.

"What's going on?" he asked, slurring his speech.

Carter looked him up and down and shook his head - he was wearing nothing but a pair of very baggy boxer shorts. Both officers could smell the alcohol on his breath. It was clear that he was still half-cut from the night before.

"I'm DCI Carter and this is DI Redding." Both officers showed their warrant cards.

"What is your full name please?"

"Daniel Mutter, why?"

"We need to question you in relation to the death of Chrissie Parker, can we come in?" asked Claire.

"What! Whoa, hold on a minute. Do you have a warrant?"

Both detectives noted that he did not show any sign of remorse or surprise at the news of his partner's death.

"No, but we only want to…"

"Well, in that case, you can fuck off!"

Carter nodded. "Okay, if that's the way you want it. Daniel Mutter, you are under arrest on suspicion of murder, you do not have to say anything at this time but anything you do say may be noted and used in evidence. You have the right to see a solicitor which we can arrange when we get back to the station. Do you understand?"

"Fuck off, ya bunch of pigs. Go on, write that down ya fuckin' arsehole."

Carter laughed out loud at the humorous insult and then stood aside to allow the uniformed officers to cuff the man.

"Hold on, can I get some clothes on? I'm freezing my balls off."

Carter nodded to the two policemen, who now held one arm each. "Take him in and find something clean for him to wear. Do not touch the clothes he was wearing last night."

Claire looked around the small kitchen and immediately pointed to the muddy boots which had been kicked off at the door. "Look, boss."

Carter didn't need Claire to explain. "Right, let's get a SOCO in here."

"Yes, boss."

She turned and saw PC Campbell, standing outside. "Constable go and get one of the SOCOs, please."

The two detectives went through to the living room and immediately saw evidence of a violent struggle.

Carter went over to a small, upturned table in the corner and spotted a pool of blood underneath it. "Looks like we have found our murder scene."

Claire had a quick look for herself and nodded in agreement. "Could have been accidental? They have a fight. He pushes her over, she cracks her head on the side of the table. She doesn't wake up, so he panics. He tries to make it look like the serial killer by taking her out into the woods and bashing her with a hammer. He's carrying her on his right shoulder…"

"Hold on, his right shoulder?" asked Carter, who up until that point had agreed with everything Claire had said.

"Yes, I noticed some footprints around the victim's body. The right footprint was deeper than the left, suggesting he was holding something heavy on his right-hand side."

Carter was impressed. "Right, and so he carries her body into the wooded area and then smashes her head open with a hammer to make it look like our serial killer."

"Yes, and he comes back to the house but instead of cleaning up the evidence, he has another drink to calm his nerves and another… and another until he drinks himself into a stupor – hence why we couldn't wake him up earlier. And when he finally does get up… I'm thinking that he may have forgotten about his actions from the previous night. He might even have thought it was all a dream, until of course, you tell him that Chrissie is dead and his first reaction is to ask about a warrant."

"All sounds very plausible, detective."

"Yip. All we need to do now is prove it."

"Yes, well, like I said, that's a job for DCI Mitchell. We need to focus on the serial killer. Clearly, this is not our guy."

"Yes, sir," she said disappointedly, unable to hide her irritation.

Chapter 33

An hour or so later, Claire headed back home on foot via the cycle path. She needed to take a shower and put on some fresh clothes before going to work for the 8 a.m. briefing. She crossed the wee bridge over the burn and entered Silverton Avenue, where she noticed a man standing on the opposite side of the road, looking as if he was waiting for someone.

He had been waiting for someone – Claire, and had been caught in a state of surprise when she unexpectedly entered the street via the bridge.

Stupid!

Thinking that he must be one of the neighbours that she still had to meet, Claire gave him a friendly wave and said hello as she passed. He gave an awkward reply of 'hello' back and immediately turned and headed down the street towards Glasgow Road. Claire thought nothing of it and made her way back into the house.

Peter was up and having his breakfast in the kitchen. She popped her head in the kitchen door to announce her return and to let him know that she would be upstairs, having a shower.

Twenty minutes later Claire came bouncing down the stairs and entered the kitchen. Peter had just finished cleaning up his dishes and was listening to the local radio describing the scene at East End Park.

Claire walked over to Peter and kissed him on the cheek. "Sorry if I disturbed you earlier."

"What? Nah, I was half awake anyway. I take it you were in the park this morning."

"Yes, but it's not what they think," she said, nodding to the radio. "It wasn't the serial killer; it was the boyfriend."

"Really? How can you be so sure?" he asked, curious to find out more.

"Trust me, we know. It's just a matter of time before he confesses – we've got a stack of evidence."

Peter shook his head in disbelief. "Well, there's nothing stranger than people!" he said, struggling to think of anything better to say.

"Talking of which, you're going to have to introduce me to some of the neighbours," said Claire.

"What do you mean?"

"Well, there was a man standing outside, across the road, and when I said hello to him, well… he seemed a bit uncomfortable about it. You know – a bit awkward. Probably because we've never been introduced."

"What did he look like?"

Claire tried to get a clear picture of the man in her head before describing him. "He was about 5ft 10, medium build, brown hair, brown eyes, wore a black woollen hat and black jacket…" She paused. "Come to think of it, I think I might have passed him yesterday at the Post Office on my way home, so he must be local."

"I can't think of any of our neighbours who match that description. Maybe he was just passing through the street."

"Maybe, but he looked like he was waiting for someone, but perhaps I'm wrong."

"Well, next time you see him, go up to him and introduce yourself," said Peter.

"What! March up to a stranger and say, 'Hi, I'm Claire. What's your name?'"

Peter laughed. "Okay, point taken. Next time you see him, let me know and I'll see if I recognise him. Anyway, I'll need to go or I'll be late."

Claire checked her watch. "Is that the time? I'll need to get going soon." She strode over to Peter and helped him put on his overcoat. "Have a good day, love."

"You too," said Peter, and kissed her on the cheek. "Let me know what time you'll be home and I'll get dinner ready."

"Probably around six, but I'll let you know if anything changes, bye love."

Peter grabbed his bag and headed for the door.

~

He saw Peter leave the house and noted the time. It wouldn't be long before she would leave for work, but clearly she could be called out at any time. He would not make that mistake again.

Chapter 34

Claire had made her way to the station in just enough time to hear DCI Carter brief the team on the morning's events and confirm that DCI Mitchell would take over the investigation. He explained, much to the relief of his team, that he and DI Redding were convinced that the murder had been staged, albeit rather clumsily, to appear like their serial killer. He also advised that there would be a press conference at 9.00 a.m. where the information would be shared with the public to allay any further rumours of a fourth serial killing. He told the team that DSup Milligan would attend the press conference to answer questions on this investigation and had asked for an update on any progress.

Brian was the first to speak. "Sir, I've just received confirmation from Coatbridge CID that they've found the file with the Coatdyke CCTV footage."

The anger that Carter had felt the previous night had dissipated and he took the news as a positive. "Right then. Monty, I want you and Patsy to go over the recordings with a fine tooth comb. You know who we are looking for, so let me know as soon as you find anything useful."

Woody spoke up next. "Boss, I've been through the file twice and cannot find DI Davidson's handover notes. They're just not there."

"Right … well … at least we didn't miss them, so that's something. Anything else to report? No? Okay, let's get on with it then."

Chapter 35

He heard the news of the fourth hammer killing on the radio and was somewhat bemused and pleased by the media speculation that the hammer killer had struck again. Clearly, someone out there had decided to copy his method of attack, which he surmised would only make the work of the police more difficult.

When the newsfeed from the radio ended, he immediately turned on his television set and searched the live news channels to see if they had any more information on the murder. After a few minutes, he noticed that the BBC News Channel was showing live footage from East End Park, Dumbarton; the scene of the fourth hammer killing. The young female reporter, who was clearly very excited at the prospect of appearing on the national news, was standing outside the police perimeter describing the scene over-enthusiastically. The TV camera moved away from the reporter, who continued with the live commentary and panned across the woods to where the body had been found and then zoomed in on the white SOC tent, which was still a hive of activity. As the camera focussed on one of the SOCOs, who had just left the tent, the reporter speculated that the unnamed victim had been brutally attacked on her way home. The young reporter added that the body had been found by a dog and that it was thought that a hammer had also been found at the scene, fuelling the speculation that this was now the scene of the fourth hammer killing!

The external TV broadcast was abruptly interrupted by the studio presenter, who announced that they would now join the police news conference, which was being held in Dumbarton Police HQ and was just about to start.

A stock photo image of the entrance to the Police Scotland HQ at Overtoun appeared on the TV screen, and then the camera shot faded into the press conference, where the BBC Scotland reporter had positioned himself at the front and centre of the media area. The camera focussed on the BBC reporter, who stopped speaking as soon as the police deputation entered the room. One by one, the senior police officers sat at the table and prepared themselves for the inevitable onslaught of questions.

Assistant Chief Constable Blackford stood up and opened the conference by introducing all the other senior officers at the table. She continued, "Detective Chief Inspector Mitchell will now make a brief statement about this morning's sad events in East End Park and then you will be given the opportunity to ask some questions. Chief Inspector Mitchell..."

DCI Mitchell picked up her script and looked up at the gallery of cameras, microphones and reporters facing her. This was not her first press conference by any means, but she was nervous and her hands shook a little as she started to speak. "Ladies and gentlemen, it is with the deepest regret that I have to confirm that the body of a 33-year-old woman was found dead in a wooded area of East End Park, Dumbarton, at approximately 0530 hours, this morning. The victim, who lived nearby, has been positively identified by a neighbour but as we have been unable to contact her immediate family, whom we believe may be abroad, we will not be able to identify her at this time. It does appear that the victim was attacked with a hammer, as has already been reported in press and media, but we are satisfied that this is not the work of the serial killer that Superintendent Mulholland of the Major Incident Team is currently pursuing and therefore this unfortunate death is completely unrelated to the other killings. I can confirm that a 34-year-old man has been arrested and is being questioned in connection with this murder. That is all the information that I can share with you at this time. Thank you."

As soon as DCI Mitchell stopped speaking, a number of hands were raised by reporters, keen to ask their question first. ACC Blackford looked around the room and pointed to the smartly dressed reporter from Sky News, indicating that he could ask his question first.

"DCI Mitchell. How can you be absolutely sure that the four deaths are unrelated?"

DCI Mitchell had anticipated this question and was comfortable in her response. "I am not able to provide any details on that at this time but can confirm that there are some clear differences between the first three murders and the fourth murder. These differences are significant enough for me to say, with some confidence, that this killing is not related to the first three murders."

As soon as the DCI stopped speaking, more hands were raised. The ACC looked around and picked out the BBC Scotland reporter in the middle of the room.

"Chief Inspector, we understand that the *victim's partner* is being held in custody in connection with her death. Can you confirm this to be the case?"

DCI Mitchell hesitated and turned towards ACC Blackford for some assistance.

ACC Blackford responded. "As previously stated, a man has been arrested in relation to the murder of the fourth victim and is currently being questioned. It would not be appropriate for him to be named at this stage in the investigation as no charges have been made yet."

The reporter was quick to respond. "So that's a yes, then. One more question, if I may, Ms Blackford?

The ACC did not look pleased with his assumption or the use of 'Ms' when addressing her, and growled, "Go on."

Everyone in the room noted her annoyance.

The reporter ignored her scowl and continued. "What progress, if any, have your officers made in relation to the investigation of the first three murders? It's been a number of days now since the body of Sheila Maxwell was found and it seems to me that you appear to be clueless."

ACC Blackford ignored the insult, smiled at the BBC Reporter and calmly turned towards Detective Superintendent Milligan and invited him to respond to the question.

"Thank you for your question," Milligan responded, buying himself a little more time to gather his thoughts. "The investigation is progressing well and we are currently following up on several leads."

"Do you have a suspect?" shouted another reporter from the back of the room.

Milligan knew that the honest answer was 'no' but was reluctant to give any type of negative response, as per his media training. "We have a number of persons of interest and, as I have already said, we are pursuing several leads…"

"But no main suspect?" shouted out another voice from the back of the room. This outburst was followed by another volley of questions from all over the room. ACC Blackford decided enough was enough and shouted over the crowd. "Settle down, settle down, we have time for one more question. Right, you over there, yes you."

She pointed to a rather portly, red-faced reporter from the Daily Record, who was sitting quietly in the corner. It was a mistake, as the wily old reporter had been biding his time, waiting for the right moment to mix things up just enough to get a reaction.

"Superintendent Milligan, what happens if there's another murder while you are all twiddling your thumbs, looking into these so-called persons of interest?"

It was one of those questions that was impossible to answer positively. The mood change in the room was palpable as the lions waited for their prey to reveal a weakness, thus allowing feeding time to begin.

ACC Blackford, being the most senior officer in the room, took it upon herself to respond to the question. "I can assure you that we are doing everything we possibly can to apprehend the killer. We're pursuing a number of..."

"Sorry, but that's a politician's response," said the reporter, smelling blood. "Answer the question, what happens if someone else dies? Who's to blame?" There were some shouts of 'clueless' across the room as the situation became even more heated than before.

ACC Blackford had had enough and exploded at the top of her voice. "The killer is to blame - that's who. He's out there now, probably watching this farce... laughing his bloody head off!"

She knew instantly that she had made a huge mistake. Without saying another word, she stood up and left the room and was followed quickly by the other officers at the table, leaving the poor police press officer behind to pick up the pieces. The room was buzzing with noise and excitement - they had their headline.

The BBC Reporter made a few brief remarks directly into the camera before the director instructed the live feed to return to the studio for further analysis.

~

ACC Blackford had been right about one thing - the killer was watching. He wasn't actually laughing out loud, but he was pleased that the police investigation appeared to be going nowhere. It was obvious they had nothing solid, so he could relax a little. His plan had worked. He had waited long enough and had executed it well, but now the real question was - how long could he wait until his next kill? He could feel the hunger growing.

Chapter 36

Claire and Carter sat staring at the small TV screen, wondering what the hell was happening.

Carter was the first to speak. "Oh shit. The ACC has lost the plot."

"Yes, well, I suppose we better get on and look into all of these so-called 'leads. And what was that about persons of interests?" said Claire.

"Well, I suppose we still have to identify the man in the long coat. He would be a person of interest if we knew who he was," Carter offered.

"Yes, let's hope we get a better look at him in Coatdyke. In the meantime, I have a few things that I want to check out this morning unless you have something else for me, sir," said Claire.

"No, go ahead, but keep me informed Claire. Milligan will want to be kept up to speed on everything we've got after that little shit show."

"Indeed!" said Claire. Carter went over to check with Monty, who was reviewing the Coatdyke CCTV.

A call came in on one of the landlines and Woody immediately picked it up. "DS Greenwood, can I help you? What? Where? Right, don't do anything. We're on the way. No, don't let him out of your sight. If he leaves the train, follow him, but do not attempt to stop him. Understand? Right, good. We'll be in touch." Woody hung up the phone and immediately crossed the room to where Carter was sitting with Monty.

"Boss, there's been a sighting on a train."

"Our man with the long coat?"

"Yes, boss. The Transport Police have eyes on him on the train to Edinburgh. They think he got on at Hyndland."

"Where's the train now?"

"Heading to Charing Cross."

"Christ, that's 30 minutes away. We'll never catch it up. Right, we're going to need the Transport Police to arrest him."

"But I thought the advice was for them not to intervene…"

"Yes, but we can't risk losing him. What if he gets off at Queen Street? No, we can't risk it. Call them back and tell them to make the arrest. We'll meet them at Queen Street as soon as we can. Tell them no one speaks to him until I get there. Got it?"

"Got it, boss." Woody headed back to the phone to make the call.

Claire was already on her feet, heading for her coat when Carter stopped her. "Claire, I want you to stay here and follow up on those leads you mentioned. I'll handle this. Rambo, come on, get your coat."

"But I thought we were going to…" said Claire, before being cut off by Carter.

"I know, but given… your condition, it's better that you stay put. Rambo and I can deal with this. It could be a false alarm for all we know. No, you take charge here and keep me informed of any developments."

Claire was raging but knew arguing with the DCI would be pointless. She went over to Woody who had finished speaking to the Transport Police. "Can I see the transcript of the interview with Robert Baird?"

Woody sensing the tension in the room, nodded without reply and fetched the file. "Here you are. There's his first interview with you and DS O'Neill and this is the one with DCI Carter and DSup Milligan." He handed the buff-coloured folder over to Claire.

"Thanks, Woody." Claire returned to her desk and dumped herself down on the chair and then opened the typed transcript. She was keen to know just how strong an alibi he had. *How could he even remember what he was doing that far back*! She could barely remember what she had done last week, never mind months ago. She read quickly through the transcript until she reached the questions on Baird's whereabouts on the other two deaths. Baird's alibi on the day of Jackie Ross's death was as solid as it could be. He was at home with Sheila and some friends on 19 November 2019; it was Sheila's birthday which made it easy for him to remember, even though it was more than a year ago. Claire read on and could see that Baird's alibi on 4th April 2020 was an unusual one; he and Sheila had been on a Zoom call with Christine, Sheila's other daughter, and that this had been checked. *Of course, it was during the first lockdown!* Claire remembered that she had to do the same thing with her parents when it was her birthday. And suddenly, a thought occurred to Claire. *What if…?*

Chapter 37

Carter and Rambo parked outside Queen Street station and headed straight for the administration block where the prisoner was being held. The double flight of stairs up to the British Transport Police offices were easy for the young Rambo who practically skipped his way up, two at a time. However, they proved much more difficult for Carter, who was out of breath by the time he reached the top. *Next time he would wait for the lift.*

They arrived at the reception area and flashed their warrant cards at the young receptionist who had been waiting for their arrival. He took them through to the back office without any delay. They were then taken to the holding cell, where the prisoner was waiting for them.

Carter entered the room first, followed by Rambo. The man in the long coat stood up as they entered. Carter took one look at him and turned around without saying a word. Rambo was stunned by Carter's behaviour and duly followed his boss back out of the cell to the corridor where two officers from the Transport Police were waiting.

The taller of the two officers, who had three stripes on his arm to indicate the rank of Sergeant, looked at Carter as if he had a set of horns on his head. "What's going on? Aren't you going to interview him?"

"Are you the arresting officer?" growled Carter.

"Well, technically no, it was PC Collins who made the arrest."

"But you were with him at the time? Yes?"

"Yes, so..."

"And what was the description that you were given?"

"Well, we were told to look out for a middle-aged man, with dark hair and a long coat."

"And?" prompted Carter.

"And what?" replied the Sergeant.

"And what fuckin' height were you given?"

"Oh, I see, eh...m, approximately six feet tall."

"Aye, and does that fuckin' dwarf in there look like he's approximately six feet tall to you Sergeant?"

Carter answered the question before the beleaguered officer could respond "Naw, he fuckin' doesn't. So, thank you for wasting my time. I'm in the middle of a fuckin' triple murder investigation!" he shouted.

The young PC next to the Sergeant interjected. "But he was sitting down when we…"

"Sitting down, sitting fuckin' down!" shouted Carter, this time at the top of his voice. Even Rambo took a step back, such was the ferocity of the verbal attack.

A door opened at the end of the corridor and a senior ranking officer from the British Transport Police came marching out demanding to know what all the noise was about. Carter was more than ready to tell him all about it.

Chapter 38

Woody put down the phone and was clearly agitated. He shouted across the room to his DI, who was deep in thought and seemed oblivious to what was going on.

"Claire, DCI Carter's on his way back and he's absolutely raging," said Woody.

"I take it that the suspect was not our man," she said calmly.

"Not even close. Apparently, he was only 5ft 6."

"And the Transport Police didn't know this?" asked Claire.

"Yeah, they did, but apparently the man was seated so they couldn't see how tall he was."

Claire laughed out loud. "I can only imagine Carter's response to that little gem. On a more positive note, I think I might be onto something else. Do you have Robert Baird's contact number on file?"

"Yes, I'm sure we'll have it somewhere. Give me a minute and I'll look it out."

"Thanks." Claire turned around and saw Brian sitting beside Monty. Both men were peering at the Coatdyke CCTV footage. "Do you have anything?" she asked.

Brian turned and responded. "Yip, we think we've got him. Same coat, same build but unfortunately the image is low quality… again!"

Claire leaned over his shoulder to take a closer look at the screen. "Yip, same build, same stance, and he's wearing trainers. It's the same guy that followed Sheila Maxwell out of Craigendoran station. Well, at least we know for sure that we're chasing the right man. If only we could identify him."

"They really need to get better lighting at these stations. There's no point spending money on CCTV if you can't get a decent image at night time," said Brian.

Claire nodded in agreement. "These are the same people that can't even get trains to run when leaves fall on the track… and you expect them to buy decent CCTV?"

"Good point, boss."

"Here's the number," said Woody, handing Claire a small Post-it note.

"Thanks, Woody."

"No problem. Why do you want to speak to Baird?" he asked.

"I've just got a hunch about something and want to check it out."

Brian couldn't help but overhear her response. "So, what's your hunch then? You're not back to thinking it's Baird again – he's definitely not the guy on the CCTV."

Claire looked at Brian and then Woody, both waiting anxiously for a response and then she smiled. "Patience gentlemen, I need to check something out first and then I'll share my thoughts with you. I promise. In the meantime, back to work!"

Claire could hear the sound of huffing and puffing coming from the two men as she turned around and went out into the corridor. She made the call to Baird, confirmed her suspicions, and then headed straight to the CID office to see DC Armstrong.

~

DC Jim Armstrong was sitting at his desk speaking on the telephone when Claire entered her old office. "Well mate, we'll be glad to get you back. It's been mayhem here ever since Sarge and the boss were seconded to MIT. Hold on, speak of the devil, she's just walked in - I'd better go. See you later, Paul. Take care." Jim put down the receiver.

Claire immediately picked up on the conversation. "How's he doing?"

"Brand new. He expects to be back to work on Monday."

"That's great news. How have things been in here?"

"Really busy and worse now we've been handed the Chrissie Parker case."

"Yeah, but that one must be done and dusted by now."

"Well, it would have been if you lot had a warrant to enter her house. Mutter's solicitor has already submitted a complaint and has alerted the Fiscal to the news that he'll be challenging all the evidence gathered inside the house on the basis of it being an illegal entry and search. We're arguing that entry was necessary to check if any further lives were at risk but I'm not sure the Fiscal will buy that one."

"What about my request for a warrant? Was it approved?"

"Oh yeah, but as it had not been issued at the time of entry, it doesn't count."

"Great. So, the whole thing could be thrown out of court on a technicality. Something else for the press to go to town on!"

"I know, did you see the conference? What a bloody fiasco!"

"Yeah, I can't believe the ACC lost it." Claire chuckled. "But it was funny!"

"Yeah, anyway, what can I do you for?" asked Jim.

Claire sat down at the empty desk opposite him. "Do you remember when we interviewed Iain Livingstone, Sheila Maxwell's ex-husband?"

"Yeah. But isn't he off the hook because you are looking for a serial killer and didn't he also have an alibi for the time of her murder? "

"Yes, that's why I'm here, Jim. Did you ever follow up on the cinema ticket?"

Jim's face went pale. "No, I thought it wasn't necessary. You had ruled him out."

"It's okay, Jim. I'm not looking to blame anyone or anything like that. It's just that some new information has come to my attention and we need to be absolutely sure that he was at the cinema when he said he was."

"Right. I'll get onto it now. Give me a few minutes."

"Thanks, Jim." Claire turned and headed back to the MIT incident room where Brian and Woody were waiting anxiously, keen to find out what she was up to.

Claire entered the room and held up her hands as if to show they were empty. "Patience gentlemen. Patience. All will be revealed in good time. I'm still checking out a few things."

They both grumbled and returned to their desks.

Chapter 39

Jim came into the incident room smiling - he had the look of a man who had just lost a pound but found a fiver. Claire, who was seated at the back of the room, spotted him and waved her hand to draw his attention. He came striding over to her to share what he thought was good news.

"Right boss, I got through to the cinema and they confirmed that the ticket was issued to a Mr Iain Livingstone. Apparently, he paid by debit card at the point of booking his seats at the cinema fifteen minutes before the movie started."

"Oh, so he didn't buy it online then?" Claire asked disappointedly.

"No, they are sure he was at the cinema and purchased the ticket before the movie commenced. They also said that they have CCTV cameras at their ticket desks and, given that we have an accurate time stamp of when he purchased the ticket, it would be quite easy to find him on video."

"Right," said Claire. "I suppose this only proves that he was there at that particular time but still worth checking out."

"Do you want me to…?"

"No, you've enough on your plate. Thanks, Jim. That's extremely helpful. I'll get someone from this team to look into it. And don't worry, I should have made sure we followed up on the alibi - it's on me, okay?"

"Thanks, boss. I hope you get the bugger, whoever he is."

"Yeah, me too, and sooner rather than later."

Claire returned to the incident room and was now in two minds about what to do next. She knew she had to follow up on Livingstone's alibi to eliminate him from the enquiry but also knew that Carter would not want to hear about her new theory. She decided to call Professor Tannock, but before Claire got the chance to pick up the phone, Brian approached her desk.

"Well, are you able to share your theory now that you've spoken with Jim?"

Claire smiled up at her colleague. "It's really getting to you, isn't it?"

He nodded.

"Okay, here goes…" Before Claire could explain her theory, Carter and Rambo stormed into the room. Carter looked around and headed straight for Claire. Brian decided to return to his seat - he could tell Carter was upset and didn't want to get in the way of the crossfire.

"What a bloody waste of time, bloody morons," said Carter as he approached Claire.

"I heard. I assume you gave them hell," she said.

"Yeah, and the rest. Anyway, do you have anything new for me?"

Claire hesitated and then decided to be brave. "Sorry sir, but I've got a bit of a confession to make. You'll remember Sheila Maxwell's ex-husband, Iain Livingstone. His alibi was that he was at the cinema."

Carter sat down, preparing himself for the worst. "Yes, what about it?"

"Well, we … no, I didn't follow up on it."

Carter's face looked like he was about to blow a fuse. "Go on."

"As you know, he presented a ticket stub as evidence that he was at the cinema in Glasgow at the time of the murder. And, before you say it, I know I should have contacted the cinema to confirm it but… well, when it was decided that we were looking for a serial killer and…"

Carter cut her off. "Oh, come on Claire, so you're now telling me he didn't attend the cinema."

"No, quite the opposite. We now know that he did buy the ticket at the cinema using his debit card fifteen minutes before the movie started and has probably been captured on CCTV." Claire was careful not to mention Jim's role in the investigation.

"Right, so it couldn't have been him then," prompted Carter. "I'm confused."

"Well, I still think it's worth checking the CCTV to confirm that he was there in person."

Carter looked perturbed. "Listen, Claire, firstly you are convinced it was personal and had to be Baird and now… what? Do you think it's this man, Livingstone? Even if his alibi isn't 100% solid, what's the connection?"

Claire paused to select the correct words but before she had time to explain Carter cut her off. "Right, so it's just a hunch. A gut feeling."

"Well, yes, which is why I also wanted to speak to Professor Tannock again. To ask some more questions about this type of killer."

"Well, if you feel you must. It certainly won't do any harm to check the CCTV but I'm not convinced the professor will be able to shine any more light on this guy". He paused to gather his thoughts and made a decision. "Okay, get Monty to contact the cinema and we'll have a look, but I'm pretty sure this is a dead end."

"I hope so, but it was my mistake and I want to be absolutely sure," explained Claire.

Carter nodded approvingly. He admired Claire for admitting her mistake, there weren't many officers who would have done the same thing – including him.

"There's something else, sir," said Claire tentatively.

Carter raised his left eyebrow. "Another mistake?"

"No. Well, maybe more of an oversight. Well, not an oversight as such, more of a communication issue."

"Get to the point, Inspector." Carter's patience was beginning to run out.

Claire realised that she was only making matters worse by dancing around the issue. "Let me explain and hopefully you'll get where I'm coming from. So, I was looking through the files, searching for a connection between the murders and I think I might have stumbled onto something important. Something that we all missed the first time around."

Carter wasn't sure if he wanted to hear any more unwelcome news but prompted Claire to proceed. "Go on."

"Well, I was curious to understand how Baird was able to give such strong alibis to the first two murders."

"I don't understand, what exactly are you getting at?" he asked.

"You may recall, there was a mention of a video call between Baird, Maxwell and their daughter Christine on 4 April."

"Yes, I remember," said Carter, showing his annoyance.

"And that was on Christine's birthday." Claire waited for Carter to process that piece of information.

"What? That wasn't... but ... oh, shit!" Carter realised his mistake.

"Sorry sir, but it's understandable. You and DCI Mitchell were simply seeking an alibi, and Woody checked it out later. Neither of you were looking for a connection to the killings at the time. No one thought to ask what the Zoom call was about. It wasn't relevant. It was only because I was looking for the connection that I stumbled upon it. Even I missed it the first time I read it."

"Even you, detective?" Carter grumbled.

"Sorry sir, didn't mean it that way."

"Fuck! How am I going to explain this one to Milligan? All three women were killed on the birthdays of Sheila Maxwell and her daughters, so they are linked in a way which can only point to Baird or Livingstone. And, as Baird has alibis for all three murders, it couldn't be him which explains why you are now so keen to establish if Livingstone's alibi stands up."

Claire was relieved that Carter now had the full picture, warts and all. "Yes sir, but let's not worry about Milligan for now. All that matters is that we nail down the case against Livingstone and get him into custody as soon as possible."

"Hold on a minute, Claire. You've seen Livingstone face to face. How could you not identify him from the CCTV footage or even from the description given by the witnesses?"

"Sir, the Iain Livingstone that I interviewed was blonde with blue eyes. None of the witnesses gave that description, and don't forget that he was wearing a mask when caught on camera. What's more, the image quality was so bad we couldn't use it, so I hardly think that…"

"Okay, okay, calm down. You're right, Claire. Sorry, I'm just annoyed at myself for missing it. So, what do you think now? That he's using a disguise, dying his hair?"

"That's my hunch, sir. Of course, we don't really know that it was him. All we really have by way of evidence is the birthdays and that could be a coincidence."

"I don't believe in coincidences, Inspector, do you?"

"No sir, but I reckon the Fiscal will want something more to go on before any charges are pressed," said Claire.

"And I wouldn't blame them. The bit I still don't get is his motive to kill the three women. Okay, even if he did hold some sort of insane grudge against his ex-wife, Sheila. Why kill the others?"

"That's what I wanted to speak to Professor Tannock about. Bring her up to speed with the birthdays and see what she thinks and … hold on … that's it!"

"What now?" asked Carter.

"What if he wanted us to think that it was the work of a serial killer to put us off the scent? And let's face it. We started looking elsewhere as soon as the three murders were linked by the same make and model of the hammer, which he deliberately left at the scene to ensure that the police linked all three crimes."

Carter knew that Claire was onto something. "You're right. He's been leading us up the garden path the whole time…"

"And we have been more than happy to follow," said Claire. "And guess what has just occurred to me?"

"What?"

"Livingstone lives within walking distance of Knightsbridge Street. He wouldn't need to get a taxi home after killing Jackie Ross."

Carter had heard enough. "Right then." He turned around and called Monty over and instructed him to get the CCTV from the cinema as a matter of urgency. Claire told Monty to contact DC Armstrong to get the cinema details. Carter then called over to Woody, who promptly came over and sat down beside them. Carter quickly explained their new line of enquiry to Woody, whose face dropped when he realised their initial oversight but perked up when told the new plan of attack.

"Oh, by the way, any news on those taxi companies?" Carter asked.

Woody shook his head. "Nothing. We have checked with them all and none have a record of any hire in that area about the time of the murder."

"Thought so," said Carter. "Okay, Claire, once we've checked out his alibi, we'll need to get Livingstone in for further questioning. In the meantime, I want eyes on him at all times. Woody, get Rambo and Patsy to start the surveillance right now. Go to his home and confirm that he's there and follow him everywhere he goes, especially if he goes near a train station."

Claire checked the time on her watch. "He's probably still at work. I'm sure he said he was a bank manager somewhere in Glasgow - the notes from the meeting will be in the file."

"Right," said Carter. "We'll double-check that and watch his movements until we're ready to bring him in. Well done, Claire, but don't get too cocky - this all falls apart if we can't break his alibi."

Claire knew that she had taken a bit of risk revealing her theory on Livingstone before having checked out his alibi but she could not ignore her gut feeling and the longer it took to bring him in, the greater the risk that he would kill again.

Carter stood up and headed for the door. "Well, it's time I gave the Super an update on where we are. Wish me luck!"

"Do you think that's a good idea, sir?" said Claire. "Is it not better to wait until we have checked out the alibi first? Just in case I'm completely wrong."

Carter paused to think about it and could see that Claire had a point. "Okay then, we'll hold off sharing this until we know about the alibi."

Chapter 40

An hour had passed since Claire had revealed her suspicions about Livingstone to Carter. The waiting around for the alibi to be confirmed was killing her. Monty had decided to go straight to the cinema to check the CCTV on site, as the cinema staff had advised that they were unable to send the files electronically – something to do with the size of the file and their email server capacity. Had Rambo been around, he could have set up a secure file transfer to the Police server, but he was already on his way to find Livingstone.

That news and the fact that Rambo and Patsy had failed to find Livingstone at his workplace (according to bank staff he was on leave) was troubling Claire. The two detectives were now headed toward his home to see if Livingstone was there but that wasn't guaranteed. The incident room fell quiet as the office phone rang loudly in the corner, demanding to be answered. Woody was the first to react and lifted the phone.

"MIT, can I help…"

"Hi Woody, it's Monty."

"Hi Monty, what do you have?"

As soon as Claire heard Monty's name she jumped up from her seat and went over to Woody to listen in to the conversation.

Monty was standing in the cinema office staring at the small CCTV monitor. "He was definitely here before the movie started, there's a clear image of him at the ticket desk."

Wooded immediately relayed the information to Claire who took the receiver and spoke to Monty. "Hi Monty, can you see what he was wearing?" she asked.

"Yes, looks like a coat."

Claire's hopes lifted. "Can you see his feet? Is he wearing trainers?"

"Sorry, I only have a shot of him waist up due to the ticket counter."

"Right," Claire paused to think. "Okay, what colour is his hair?"

"Impossible to say, he's wearing a hat," replied Monty.

"Well, that's rather convenient," said Claire.

"What do you mean?" asked Monty.

"Because I am convinced he's dying his hair to disguise himself. Livingstone has blonde hair –

or at least he did when I interviewed him," she explained.

"Oh right, well, at least we have confirmation that he was here. What else do you want me to do now?" asked Monty.

"Are there any cameras watching the doors? It's important we confirm when he actually left the cinema. All we have is proof that he bought a ticket."

Monty relayed the question to the cinema manager who was helping him review the footage.

"There are four cameras, one for each exit, so it could take me some time to check all four sets of videos. Is that what you want me to do?" asked Monty.

"Sorry, Monty, I'm afraid it's necessary."

"Okay, I'll let you know if I find anything," he replied and hung up.

Claire looked around the room. "Woody, where's Carter gone?"

"Don't know. He's probably…" Woody stopped mid-sentence as Carter entered the room. He noticed Claire and Woody and immediately called them over to his desk.

"So, what's happening? Any news?" asked Carter.

"Monty has confirmed that Livingstone was present at the cinema to purchase the ticket," said Claire.

"Oh! So where does that leave us?" asked Carter.

"Well, Monty was also able to confirm that Livingstone was wearing a coat and a hat."

Carter picked up on the significance of the hat. "To disguise his hair colour."

"Yes, so it's still possible that Livingstone is our man. I hope you don't mind but I've asked Monty to stay at the cinema to see if we can confirm when Livingstone left the cinema."

"Good thinking, Claire. Any news from Rambo and Patsy?"

"No sir, I was just about to give Rambo a call. They must be at his house by now."

"Don't bother, I'll do it," said Carter, picking up his phone.

"Hello, Rambo? Yeah. Any news on Livingstone's whereabouts?"

"Sorry sir, we're at his house now but there's no sign of him."

"Right, well stay there and let us know if he turns up. He must come home at some point."

"Yes boss," said Rambo, not relishing a lengthy spell of surveillance in the pool car with Patsy.

Carter hung up and shook his head at Claire and Woody. "Looks like we are going to have to wait a bit longer. Claire, on the assumption that we do bring him at some point today, let's put our heads together and prepare for the interview. I think we're going to have to use all the tricks in the book to get anything out of Livingstone."

"Like trying to get blood out a living-stone," joked Woody. No one laughed.

"Aye, very good," said Carter sarcastically.

Claire ignored Woody, "Sir, could we consult with Professor Tannock first. She might be able to suggest ways to open him up a bit."

"Yeah, let's set up a conference call."

Chapter 41

The conversation with Professor Tannock was enlightening; she had explained to the detectives that it would be exceedingly difficult to break down Livingstone's charade but if they were able to play on his arrogance or get under his skin a little, then he might reveal something they could use against him. Claire relished the challenge. However, all this was immaterial given that they didn't know where he was. He still hadn't returned home and Carter was becoming increasingly impatient. Carter had now briefed Milligan on the new developments and although Milligan was not as convinced as Carter that Livingstone was the killer, the evidence being circumstantial, he was willing to authorise the request for the warrant to search his house.

The first piece of news arrived at 4.56 p.m. A much relieved Rambo called in to confirm that Livingstone had arrived home so everything now hung on Monty. Carter decided to call Monty and see how much more of the video he had to check. The news was not good. Monty had failed to see him leave the first time around and was now double-checking each video slowly to make sure he hadn't missed him.

Carter was gutted and called Claire over to his desk to discuss what to do next. "Bad news, I'm afraid. Monty's not found anything."

"Shit! So, what do we do now?" asked Claire.

Carter held his head in both hands. "I'm tempted to gamble. Pull him in for another interview and hold him here while we search his house. It's that or we keep a surveillance team on him and hope we catch him in the act. There's risks both ways. If we pull him in then we risk giving him the heads up that we're onto him and if we don't find any evidence at his house then we may have lost our chance of ever convicting him. He might even disappear!"

Claire nodded. "Yes, and if we let him go there's always the chance that he'll lose the surveillance team and kill again and we'll be in deep shit."

Carter made up his mind. "Okay, stuff it, let's bring him in for further questioning but not under arrest."

"Yes, sir. I'll call Rambo and Patsy to do that now."

"Right, I'll go and see the Super and let him know what we're going to do."

Chapter 42

Rambo approached the door to the Georgian mid-terraced house and rang the doorbell. If the DI was correct, he was about to meet a serial killer.

If Rambo was nervous, he didn't show it. Patsy on the other hand was less than comfortable and would have preferred to be accompanied by a couple of uniformed officers, as would normally be the case. He stood directly behind Rambo, nervously biting his fingernails. The large wooden door opened and the two detectives were greeted by Livingstone, who was wearing a Paisley-patterned dressing gown and holding a small towel which he was using to dry his wet hair.

"Yes, can I help you?" he asked before either detective could speak.

"Are you Mr Iain Livingstone?" Rambo asked.

"Yes, and who are you?"

"I'm Detective Sergeant Ramnik Bahanda and this is Detective Constable Craig Paterson." Both officers showed their warrant cards to Livingstone, who took a quick glance and accepted them to be valid.

"We would like you to accompany us to Police HQ in Dumbarton for questioning regarding the murders of Grace Anderson, Jackie Ross and Sheila Maxwell," said Rambo, fully expecting a reaction and was not disappointed.

Livingstone was visibly shocked but soon regained his composure. "For questioning? So, I'm not under arrest then?" he asked.

"Yes sir. That's correct. You are not under arrest but I should inform you that a search warrant has been requested and we will need access to your premises while…"

Livingstone was quick to respond. "Oh, there's no need to wait for the warrant detective. Come on in. I've nothing to hide."

This time it was Rambo's turn to be surprised. "Right, sir. That's particularly good of you, but we won't be the ones conducting the search. HQ is sending down another team. Our job is to escort you safely to Police Headquarters where DCI Carter and DI Redding are waiting to interview you."

"Oh, DI Redding again. I suppose she must have conveniently forgotten that I already have provided an alibi for Sheila Maxwell's murder," he said sarcastically.

"It's not for me to comment or speculate on the purpose of the interview, sir," responded

Rambo, keen not to get involved in any form of discussion with Livingstone.

"Very well detective, you better come in. I suppose it's okay if I get dressed first?"

"Of course, sir," said Rambo, who was genuinely beginning to wonder if the DI was right about Livingstone. *Why would someone who was guilty be so willing to allow the police to search their premises? It didn't make any sense.*

Livingstone went upstairs to get dressed while Rambo and Patsy went into his front room to wait. Rambo decided to call the station and let them know what was happening but more importantly to tell them that Livingstone had given permission to allow his premises to be searched without a warrant which was welcome news to Carter, as he had been told that the Fiscal wasn't too happy with the lack of evidence presented by the police to justify the search. Claire quickly decided that Rambo and Patsy should wait until the search party arrived - that way the keys to the house could be handed over by Livingstone to enable the search to be conducted in his absence.

"Patsy, go and tell Mr Livingstone that there's no hurry to get dressed – we're having to wait for the search team to arrive before we can leave."

Patsy did as he was told and passed on the message to Livingstone who appeared to be neither up nor down about the slight change of plan. Livingstone did as he was asked and took his time getting ready. When he came downstairs it was obvious that he had also taken the time to shave and notably had blow-dried his blonde hair. He was wearing casual grey trousers and a black polo neck shirt as if he were going to play a round of golf.

"Can I get you gentlemen something to drink, while we wait for your colleagues to arrive?" he asked casually.

"A cup of tea …" said Patsy.

"No thank you, sir. We're fine as we are," said Rambo, glaring at Patsy.

"Suit yourselves. You don't mind if I have one, do you? I'm gasping!"

"It's your house, sir. Go ahead," said Rambo.

Livingstone went back out to the hall and turned left to go to the kitchen.

"Patsy. The next time a suspected serial killer offers you a cup of tea, think twice about it!"

"Oh, yeah. Sorry. Eh… Rambo, do you think he's guilty? He's certainly not acting like it, is he? I mean, why would he give permission for the search without a warrant if he's got something to hide."

"I know. I just hope the DI knows what she's doing."

"But it's not just the DI though, Carter's also on board."

"Yeah, but she had to persuade him. Didn't she?"

Both detectives were completely unaware that Livingstone was standing outside the door, listening to their conversation, waiting for a gap in the conversation before entering.

~

The search party, led by DS O'Neill, arrived just as Livingstone was finishing his cup of tea.

"Good timing," said Livingstone who stood up to go. I'll just fetch my jacket."

Patsy went to the door to let Brian and the other police officers into the house and waited in the hallway for Livingstone, who came bouncing down the stars as if he didn't have a care in the world.

"Mr Livingstone, this is DS O'Neill. He'll be conducting the search of your house."

"Hello, Sergeant. I hope you don't damage anything during your search. I'm not sure my insurance will cover…"

"That's okay. We'll be careful, sir. Now, if you want to hand over your keys we'll let you get on your way to the station."

"Oh, there's no need for that Sergeant. It's a Yale lock. Just close the door behind you when you leave and it should lock itself."

Brian turned around to look at the lock mechanism and nodded. "I see, it's the old fashioned kind. Okay, we'll do that. What about the backdoor?"

"I've left the key in the door. I thought you might want to go out there and look in my shed," said Livingston pointing to the kitchen.

"Thank you," Brian replied and then made his way to the backdoor where he could see the key in the lock.

"This way Mr Livingstone," said Rambo.

The three men left the house and headed to the station leaving the search party to get on with their work.

Chapter 43

Rambo and Patsy arrived in Dumbarton approximately 30 minutes after leaving Livingstone's home in Jordanhill. The twenty-minute journey had taken longer than usual due to a lane closure on the A82, a common occurrence on the busy highway.

The two detectives escorted Livingstone to Interview Room 1, where DCI Carter and DI Redding were waiting to receive him. Carter had invited Professor Tannock to observe the interview and accordingly, she and DSup Milligan were waiting in the room next to the interview room, ready to observe via the audio/video feed. The screen was split into two: one half focused on the two detectives, the other on the empty seats opposite them.

Rambo knocked on the door to let them know he was entering and escorted Livingstone into the room. Both detectives stood up to welcome Livingstone.

"Mr Livingstone, I'm DCI Carter. I believe you have already met DI Redding."

Livingstone grinned and nodded, "Yes, how could I forget."

"Please take a seat," said Carter.

Livingstone did as he was asked. "Chief Inspector, before you begin, I understand that I have been brought in for further questioning but that I am not under arrest. Is that correct?"

"Yes, that's correct," Carter responded, his expression indicating that he was a little concerned about where this was going.

Livingstone continued. "Good, and I see that the cameras are on. Is this interview being recorded?"

"Yes, is that a problem? Do you object to the recording?" Carter asked.

"Oh no, on the contrary. I welcome it," said Livingstone looking directly into the camera."

Carter was taken aback by his response and gave Claire a quizzical look before continuing.

"Thank you, Mr Livingstone. So, are you happy to proceed then?"

"Yes, and just so we are all clear, I am here voluntarily. I have agreed that my home be searched by the police without a warrant. In other words, I am more than happy to assist you with your investigation and have already demonstrated that I have cooperated in full."

Again, Carter was taken by surprise. "Right, well thank you, Mr Livingstone. As you know, we are now investigating the murder of two other women, Grace Anderson and Jackie Ross, in addition to the murder of your ex-wife."

"Yes, your Sergeant mentioned it," Livingstone replied casually, "but forgive me for interrupting - aren't you looking for a serial killer? Someone who killed all three women."

"Yes."

"So, it couldn't possibly be me as I've already given DI Redding here details of my whereabouts when Sheila Maxwell was murdered."

Claire sensed Carter's hesitation. *Come on Carter, keep going, ignore him and stick to the plan!*

"I was going to raise that later in the interview but since you have brought it up, we might as well address it now. Since your first interview, we have been able to confirm that you purchased a ticket at the cinema but that's not proof that you stayed on to watch the full movie."

"So, on the basis that you can't confirm my alibi, I must be guilty. Is that it, detective?"

Carter was beginning to lose patience with Livingstone. "No one has accused you of anything yet, Mr Livingstone."

Claire decided it was time to intervene and steer them back to the original plan. "Do the dates, 4 April and 19 November mean anything to you, Mr Livingstone?" she asked.

"Of course, they are the dates of the girls' birthdays; Christine and Irene."

"And can you remember where you were between the hours of 10 p.m. and midnight on 4 April 2020 and 15 November 2019?"

"I've no idea but I was probably in bed at that time of night, why?" responded Livingstone.

"Because that was when Jackie Ross and Grace Anderson were murdered. A bit of a coincidence don't you think?"

"Oh, I see where this is going," said Livingstone, sneering at Claire.

Claire sensed she was beginning to get to him and decided to go a step further. "And would it surprise you to know that we have CCTV footage of you at Coatdyke station, getting off the same train that Grace Anderson was on before she was killed?" It was a bit of a bluff and both detectives knew it, but Claire thought it was worth trying just to see Livingstone's reaction.

For the first time during the interview, Livingstone was not as quick to respond and Claire thought that she saw a slight involuntary twitch above Livingstone's right eye. Just a flicker, but it was there.

Livingstone gathered himself. "Oh, I think you must be mistaken, detective. As I said, I was probably in bed so it couldn't have been me."

It was a good response which didn't leave Claire much room to manoeuvre. Thankfully, Carter was desperate to get back into the conversation and was ready with his next question. "So, just to be clear, Mr Livingstone. We have three murders, all with the same Modus Operandi: same murder weapon, all female victims who bear a remarkable resemblance to your ex-wife and all killed on the birthdays of your daughters and your ex-wife. That's not a coincidence, is it?"

"I don't know detective, is it? I thought it was your job to solve the crime, not speculate. I assume you don't have any actual evidence which suggests that I am the killer or you would have thrown it in my face before now. In fact, it's likely this whole interview has been deliberately set up to try and trap me even though I have fully cooperated with your investigation. You know, detective, this is beginning to feel a bit like police harassment."

"Harassment?" Carter growled back. "I'll …"

Claire intervened before Carter blew a gasket, "Let's take a little break, shall we. Would you like a cup of tea, Mr Livingstone?"

Livingstone was beaming. "I thought you'd never ask, detective. Milk with two sugars, please."

Carter and Claire left the room and immediately went into the TV room, where Milligan and Professor Tannock were sitting in silence.

Claire was the first to speak. "He's certainly playing it very cool, isn't he?"

"Yes, but did you notice the little nervous twitch when you confronted him with the CCTV footage?" asked Tannock. "That really shook him up."

"Yes," said Claire. "But he recovered well and didn't fall for our bluff."

"Bluff? You mean you don't have any CCTV footage?"

"We do, but he has disguised himself so well, we could never prove that it was him to a jury."

"And that is all you have on him other than a potential motive to kill Sheila Maxwell?"

"I'm afraid so. What do you think? Could he be our killer?"

"It's hard to say from that interview but he's certainly displaying some of the characteristics of a psychopath."

Carter had had enough. "He's a fucking arrogant prick - that's what he is. Did you hear him? Harassment?"

"That's enough Chief Inspector," said Milligan, who had been sitting quietly in the corner listening to the conversation. "The plan was to shake him up, force a mistake but he seems to have done that to you. Well, I hate to say it but unless we find something at his house, we're going to have to let him go."

"We can still arrest him and hold him for up to 24 hours. You never know, something might turn up," pleaded Carter.

"Hold him on what grounds? We have nothing other than circumstantial evidence and some poor CCTV footage. No, he's already played his cards and played them well. We need something solid to hold him on. Claire, find out how the search is going and get him a cup of tea. That'll give us a few minutes or so to decide. Oh, and Carter, I want to see you in my office." It was clear from his tone that this wasn't a request.

Claire stepped outside the room to make the call. "Hi Brian, any news?"

"Sorry boss, nothing." He sounded completely pissed off.

"Shit. Milligan's going to let him go if we don't find something soon."

"We've searched everywhere," said Brian.

"What about his shed?" asked Claire.

"That's the first place I looked. He has a full set of tools including a hammer, all organised neatly, all hanging up on a wall, everything in its place. I've never seen such an organised workspace."

Claire remembered what Professor Tannock had said about the killer – he could be good with his hands. "I take it the hammer didn't match the three we have in evidence?"

"No, it's much older, has a well-worn wooden handle."

"Right. What about the bathroom? Find any evidence of hair dye in the sink?"

"Nope, clean as a whistle."

"Shit, and no sign of any keepsakes, souvenirs? The ring, heel of the shoe…"

"Nope. Do you want us to start lifting carpets and ripping up floorboards?"

"Better not, Milligan is already worried about getting a complaint."

"Oh. Why is that?" asked Brian.

"Well, the interview didn't quite go as planned. Carter lost his temper and Livingstone accused him of police harassment. Carter's in with Milligan now, probably getting a telling off."

Brian chuckled at the thought. "So, you've got nothing then?" What about Monty? Is he still looking at CCTV from the cinema?"

"Must be or we would have heard by now."

"Boss, I hate to ask but are you sure it's Livingstone? He was very relaxed when we arrived and practically invited me to search his shed."

Claire sighed. "I'm beginning to doubt it myself to be honest, but there's something about him. Something's not right - he's too relaxed. It's as if he knows we won't find anything at the house. He's just too bloody confident to be innocent! Does that make any sense?"

"Yeah. I guess we'll need to let him go if nothing turns up."

"Yip," Claire conceded. "Looks like it. See you later, Brian," she said and then hung up. She went and got a cup of tea for Livingstone and took it to him.

"That took a long time, detective. How long are you going to keep me here *for questioning?*"

Claire did not rise to the bait. "I'm sorry, Chief Inspector Carter has been detained on another matter but I'm sure he'll be back soon. Enjoy your tea."

Claire left the room and went back into the TV room to wait for Milligan and Carter to return. Professor Tannock was sitting there writing down some notes and looked up as the detective approached. "Oh Claire, I've been thinking, why don't you try to get him to share his feelings about the divorce or the girls, see if there's something there?"

"I don't see why not. He's certainly not going to break down and confess, that's for sure."

Milligan and Carter returned. Carter's face was like a beetroot and Claire could only imagine how that conversation had gone down. "Anything at the house? Milligan asked grumpily.

"No sir, DS O'Neill asked if he should start lifting carpets and floorboards…"

"No, absolutely not!"

"That's what I told him, sir."

"Right, well I suppose we'll need to let him go but I want him watched, round-the-clock surveillance. Carter – get a team organised".

"Sir, Professor Tannock has suggested a different line of questioning which might get a reaction from Livingstone."

Milligan took a moment to consider the suggestion and then gave in. "Okay, I suppose it's worth a try."

"Right, come on Claire," said Carter.

"No, I'll go in this time. Let's see if *we* can keep cool heads," Milligan said to Claire.

Carter was seething but said nothing in response.

"Come on, James, you can sit beside me and watch the show," said Tannock, patting the seat beside her.

Carter dumped himself down onto the seat so hard that he almost fell over backwards.

It took all of her powers of self-control not to burst into a fit of laughter but Tannock knew that would make Carter's mood worse, if that was possible, and so she stared straight ahead at the small screen, refusing to look at him.

Chapter 44

Claire and Milligan entered the interview room, where Livingstone was sipping his tea.

"Finally!" said Livingstone, putting down his cup and sitting up.

"Mr Livingstone, this is Detective Superintendent Milligan," said Claire. "Chief Inspector Carter has had to attend to another matter and so we will conclude the interview."

"Conclude the interview?" asked Livingstone. "I thought it had concluded, what else do you need to ask that you haven't already covered?"

"I have just a few more questions, if you don't mind," Claire responded politely.

Livingstone looked at his watch, sucked air through his teeth and crossed his arms huffily. "Well, as long as it's only a few questions, carry on Inspector."

"Thank you. In your first interview, you confirmed that your separation and divorce were not amicable. Is that correct?"

"Yes, that's correct."

"Can you explain why that was the case?" asked Claire.

"I thought I already had. Sheila got the house and my girls."

"Right, but why did you separate in the first place? Did you have an affair?"

Livingstone's face reddened. "No detective, it was Sheila who had the affair with him, with Baird. Why are you not questioning him? He's the one who was found with blood all over him at the scene after all!"

Claire ignored Livingstone's response. She could see his temper was beginning to rise a little. She just had to keep on pushing in the hope that he would break. "And how did that make you feel? Sheila being at fault but getting to keep your home and the girls. That must have hurt?"

"Yes, it did, but I don't see what this has to do…"

"And what about the girls?" asked Claire, determined to keep pushing his buttons.

"What about them?" he growled.

"I understand they chose to stay with your mother in preference to you and refused to visit you."

"That's a fucking lie. She stopped them from seeing me. The girls had no say in the matter. Who told you that? I bet it was Baird - he's a lying bastard!" Livingstone exclaimed, his face reddening.

"Did you love your girls, Mr Livingstone?" Claire asked.

"Of course I did. What sort of question is that? Right, I have had enough of this nonsense," said Livingstone, standing up. "This is nothing but harassment, pure and simple. You're deliberately trying to goad me and I'm not having it. You either arrest me or you let me go."

Claire turned to Milligan to make the call.

"Okay, Mr Livingstone. You're free to go. I'll get an officer to escort you to the exit."

Livingstone glared at Claire. "Thank you, Superintendent. I'm glad someone here has the good sense to realise that you are barking up the wrong tree."

Claire ignored the little dig, left the room and returned with a uniformed officer who led Livingstone out of the office and down to the exit.

"I thought I almost had him there," said Claire.

Milligan nodded. "And I think he knew it, hence the sharp exit." Milligan turned to the camera. "Carter, make sure he's followed at all times. We need to get the bastard."

"So, you're convinced it's him now, sir?" asked Claire.

"Yes, we just need to be able to prove it."

Carter and Professor Tannock came into the interview room.

"I've got a team on him, sir," Carter confirmed.

"I thought you nearly had him going there, Inspector," said Tannock.

"Do you think it's him?" asked Claire.

"Please, call me Charlene. Well, one thing is for sure, he hasn't gotten over his separation but I can't help thinking that something else must have triggered the attacks. Something more recent but significant. Why wait eight years or so before doing anything about it?"

The Professor had given Claire something new to think about. "Thanks, Charlene, and it's Claire by the way, you can drop the Inspector."

"You know Claire, I think we could become good friends. Do you fancy going out for a drink sometime?"

"Yes, let's do that?" said Claire. "Maybe, after this case is over."

"Cool, I'll be in touch," said Charlene.

"Okay, well if you girls are finished being best pals, we need to get back to work," said Milligan.

Tannock took that as her cue to leave and made her way downstairs to the exit.

Claire returned to the incident room to be told that Monty had come up blank at the cinema so they couldn't prove that Livingstone had watched the whole or even part of the movie, but on the other hand he couldn't prove that he had been there the whole time either. Of course, he didn't need to prove anything. The onus was on the prosecution to do that.

Claire sat there thinking about what Charlene had said to her. *Something must have triggered him to kill. Why wait eight years?* Claire decided it was time to dig into Livingstone's background a bit more but knew there were other riddles to solve. *If he was guilty and was keeping souvenirs, where were they hidden?* If she could find the answer to these key questions, she would find a way to convict him. She was sure of it. It was only a matter of time.

Chapter 45

Claire had set her alarm to ring at 6.30 am. She had decided to go for a jog before breakfast and quickly got dressed and headed out. She put the headphone plugs into her ears and selected one of her motivational playlists on her phone. She loved jogging; it wasn't just the buzz from the endorphins that it generated, but it also allowed her to empty her head and think clearly.

She crossed the small bridge at the end of Silverton Avenue, did a few stretches and then started to jog along the cycle path towards Bowling. She was completely unaware that she was being followed. This time, the assassin had been prepared for her to leave home earlier than usual and made sure he was well out of sight. He decided to follow her but kept a good distance behind to avoid detection. She had already noticed him once; a second sighting could result in her becoming suspicious. Thankfully, he had kept himself very fit and found it relatively easy to keep up with her pace. The further along the path she ran, the more confident he became that this would be the ideal location for *the accident*. When she reached the road crossing at the Bowling roundabout, he stopped running and headed back down the cycle path. He now knew what he had to do and how to do it. It was just a matter of timing.

Claire continued running until she reached the swing park in Bowling and then turned back towards home. Throughout the length of the run, her mind had focussed on one thing – catching Livingstone. She replayed all the unanswered questions in her mind. *What was the trigger? Where did he keep the souvenirs: the long coat, the hammers, the hair dye? Why wasn't he caught on CCTV returning to Craigendoran station, as she had hoped? How did he get home from Craigendoran?* The questions kept on going round and round in her head without any answers.

Before she knew it she was home again and immediately went into the shower. As the hot water poured down on her, she relaxed and looked down at her stomach, where a small bump had started to appear. Her thoughts drifted to her pregnancy and how she would behave as a mother. She was determined that she would raise her child her own way and not the way that she was raised by her mother. Not that she had a bad upbringing, quite the opposite, but her mother was determined that her precious daughter would pursue a respectable profession as a lawyer or doctor or accountant or some other boring job and was clearly disappointed when Claire decided to join the force, having graduated with flying colours. No, she would allow her child to blossom and choose their own path unhindered by the shackles of an overprotective mother. Her thoughts returned to Livingstone again and then something suddenly occurred to her. *Why did I not think of that before?* Like every puzzle, it always seemed obvious once you knew the answer. She would need to check a few things first but if her hunch was correct, she would catch the killer.

Chapter 46

Claire strode into the incident room fifteen minutes earlier than she was due to commence work such was her enthusiasm to find out if there was any substance to her epiphany in the shower. She opened her laptop and logged into the Police server which gave her access to the electoral register. She entered 'Livingstone' and searched the Helensburgh area. Four addresses appeared on the green screen. Claire clicked on the first one to reveal the names of all persons registered at the address and quickly determined it was not the one she was looking for. She clicked on the second address and again was disappointed. *Shit!* Claire clicked on the third one and smiled. This one was hopeful. She picked up her phone and quickly typed in the name of the sole occupant into Google and got several hits. She scrolled through them until she came to the Helensburgh Advertiser and there it was, in black and white, an obituary for Marjorie Livingstone, beloved wife of the late John Livingstone and mother of Iain, her only child. Claire checked the date of death – September 2019. *Two months prior to Grace Anderson's death. He had planned the whole thing to put them off the scent and it had worked. But why was his mother's death the trigger?* That was the part of the puzzle that eluded Claire and could only be answered by Livingstone. *There must have been something more than just the death of his mother to trigger his anger and re-ignite the hatred and resentment which had been burning inside him all that time.*

"Hi Claire," said Carter as he entered the room.

Claire jumped with fright. "Don't do that! You scared the life out of me!"

Carter smiled. "What's going on? It's not like you to get in before your shift starts," he quipped.

"I think I've worked it out. I think I know where we'll find all the evidence we need to nail Livingstone once and for all."

Carter sat down beside Claire. "Go on then, don't leave me hanging."

Claire explained how her thoughts had emerged when she was in the shower. One side of her brain thinking about Livingstone, the other thinking about motherhood and suddenly it occurred to her to check if Livingstone had any relatives still living in the Helensburgh area, but more importantly, did Livingstone have access to a property. His mother's death had provided the property which he would have inherited. However, the timing of his mother's death was also significant as it was just two months before the first killing.

Carter was completely on board. "And that would explain why we didn't see him return to Craigendoran station. All he had to do was walk to his mother's house and stay there for the night."

"Yes, and he was sharp enough not to tell the Electoral Registration Office that his mother had passed away, so when I did the original search for him, only his Jordanhill address appeared," explained Claire.

"He's bloody clever, I'll give him that," said Carter, now fully appreciating the length that Livingstone had gone to deceive them.

"A classic psychopath!" said Claire.

Carter agreed. "Right, we'll need to brief Milligan on this. We still don't have any hard evidence on Livingstone and we'll need a warrant to search his mother's house."

"Will that be a problem, sir?" asked Claire.

"Will what be a problem?"

"The fact that Livingstone is not registered as living there. We don't even know if ownership has transferred to him. I'm only guessing it has, as he was the only child."

"Good point, we'll need to check the Land Register but I'm pretty sure it won't affect the search warrant - my main concern is that the Fiscal will want more evidence before authorising the search. We were lucky that Livingstone granted permission last time. He's not going to do so this time. That's for sure."

"How are the surveillance team doing, sir. Have you heard anything?"

"Not yet. Why?"

"We need to know if he's heading to Helensburgh. After yesterday, he might have taken fright and tried to clean out any evidence he's hiding at his Mum's place."

"So, we need to get there first or we're buggered," said Carter.

"Well, that's one way of putting it, but yes. We can't let him out of our sight."

"Right, I'll check with the surveillance team and then speak to Milligan. The sooner we get the search warrant the better. And, eh… good work Claire."

"Thanks, boss," said Claire, smiling to herself.

Chapter 47

Carter checked in with the surveillance team, who confirmed that Livingstone was still at home. Carter informed them that Rambo and Patsy had been assigned to the dayshift surveillance and would take over at 8 a.m. He then spoke with Milligan who reluctantly agreed to speak to the Fiscal about getting the search warrant.

Claire briefed the rest of the team about the recent developments and arranged to have some uniformed officers on standby to assist with the search. She had been assigned to lead the search, so they were all now playing a waiting game and the clock was ticking – all except Brian, who was late.

The door to the incident room opened and Claire looked up expectantly. It was Carter. "Well, did the Super agree?" asked Claire.

"Yes, but he's not confident that the Fiscal will approve it," Carter replied. "The Fiscal is still pissed off with me for entering the property at East End Park without a warrant even if it did result in an arrest. Mutter's solicitor is trying to argue that we only made the arrest after we entered the premises and discovered the blood."

"I hate to say it, but he might have a point," said Claire, fully aware that she was sticking her neck out a little.

"I know, but we didn't know who else might be in the house. There could have been children at risk… and it was just a matter of minutes before your warrant was approved."

"So, that one might need to go to the Sheriff to determine if the evidence obtained in the search was admissible?" she asked.

Carter nodded slowly. "Probably, and Mutter is less likely to confess now. Anyway, that's not our concern. We need to stop Livingstone. The sooner we get a warrant to search his mother's place, the better."

"Is Milligan aware that we need to get in there before Livingstone?" asked Claire.

"Yes, but he's more relaxed about it because we have Livingstone under surveillance. He doesn't even want to call the Fiscal until after 9 a.m. He thinks he'll have a better chance of persuading him if he calls during normal office hours."

"Right, so that's been confirmed then - we know for certain that Livingstone is still at home."

"Sorry, I should've said. Yes, he is and I've asked for an update every fifteen minutes until he leaves the house." Carter checked his watch. "In fact, Rambo should be reporting in any minute now."

Chapter 48

Brian rushed into the incident room and immediately apologised for being late. Claire could see that he was not his usual self and went over to speak to him.

"Everything okay, Brian?"

Brian was slightly out of breath after the exertion of running up the two flights of stairs to reach the CID corridor but managed to speak in between gasps. "Sorry, boss … can we go somewhere private to speak?"

"Sure, we can use one of the interview rooms," said Claire. They made their way to the first interview room which was free and sat down inside.

"Is it Agnes," asked Claire. Is she…?"

"Yes, but she's fine," Brian responded, suddenly realising that Claire had picked up the wrong end of the stick. "It's actually good news. She's getting her operation tomorrow – there was a cancellation. She had to go in this morning for tests to ensure that she'll be well enough to undergo the surgery tomorrow. That's why I was late. I hate to ask but if the operation goes ahead, could I take tomorrow off on leave?"

"Of course, you shouldn't have bothered coming today." Claire leant over and much to his surprise she gave the big man a hug.

He hugged her back gently and then slowly released her. There were tears in his eyes which he quickly wiped on his sleeve. "Thanks, boss. I'm fine for today but I know I'll be a complete waste of space tomorrow, what with the worry and…"

"It's not a problem, Brian. We'll probably have him by then, provided we get the search warrant."

"Search warrant?"

"Yes, sorry, you missed the briefing, so you won't know."

"Know what? What's happened?"

Claire spent the next five minutes bringing Brian up to speed with developments.

Chapter 49

An hour had passed, and the mood within the incident room was going downhill fast. Claire sat at her desk, waiting impatiently for the search warrant to be approved and decided that she had had enough. She had to know if Livingstone was home, and the only confirmation would be someone seeing him. She went over to Carter, who was busy typing up his justification to enter Mutter's property without a warrant. DCI Mitchell had insisted on getting his statement in writing before presenting the case to the Fiscal's Office.

"Sorry to interrupt, sir. Any news on the search warrant?"

Carter saved his work and turned to face Claire. "Nope, it turns out the Fiscal is in a meeting this morning."

"What? Sir, in that case, I think we should get Rambo to knock on Livingstone's door and confirm that he's actually there," demanded Claire.

"If we do that, he'll know we're watching him and probably submit a complaint. Remember, police harassment!"

"Yes, but I'd rather do that than risk losing our only chance of getting him."

Carter thought about it, then picked up his mobile and called Rambo.

"Hi, boss, what's up?"

"Change of plan. Go rattle his door and make sure he's in."

"Are you sure? He'll know…."

"Just do it, Rambo, and let me know as soon as possible."

Carter hung up on Rambo and returned to his statement. Claire stood there waiting for the news.

Chapter 50

Rambo and Patsy made their way to Livingstone's door and rang the doorbell. They waited for what they determined to be a reasonable amount of time before trying again. Nothing. There was no response. Rambo immediately called Carter to let him know and braced himself for the onslaught of swearing which was bound to follow.

"Hello, sir. It's me. Livingstone is not responding, what do you want us to do?"

After filling Rambo's ear with the anticipated barrage of expletives, Carter finally calmed down. Claire could tell from Carter's reaction that Livingstone was gone and immediately came up with a plan. "We need to get someone to Livingstone's mum's house immediately. He could be destroying the evidence as we speak."

Carter agreed. "Right, you and Brian go and see if he's there, but you can't go in without a warrant. Understand?"

"Yes, sir."

"Right. I'll go and demand that Milligan gets the Fiscal out of his meeting. This has changed things! He'll need to grant it now. Oh, and Claire, take a couple of uniforms with you but don't take any risks. You're pregnant, remember!"

"How could I forget, sir," she said, holding the small round bump in her tummy. She turned and called over to Brian to grab his jacket - they were going to Helensburgh.

Chapter 51

Claire and Brian had just passed through Cardross when Carter called to advise that Milligan had not managed to get a hold of the Fiscal but was trying to persuade one of his assistants to approve the warrant.

"So, what do we do if we see him in the house? Just sit there, waiting for the warrant, while he destroys the evidence?" asked Claire.

"We don't know for certain that the evidence is there, Claire. So, yes, until we get the search warrant, we sit tight. Otherwise we'll find ourselves on the wrong side of an inquiry! Understood?"

"Yes, sir, understood," Claire grumbled. She hung up the call and immediately clicked on Google Maps to enter the address of the house in Helensburgh.

"We'll be there in five minutes, Brian. Let's just pray that Livingstone is elsewhere."

"Still waiting on the warrant, then?" asked Brian.

"Yeah, still waiting." Claire turned to see if the squad car was still on their tail. "What happened to our uniforms?"

"They got stuck at the temporary traffic lights in Cardross, but they'll soon catch up."

Claire wasn't at all concerned by the absence of the squad car. They would only be needed if Livingstone refused access to the property, if and when the warrant was approved.

Their unmarked car approached the new housing scheme on the outskirts of Helensburgh and Brian. A car approached in the opposite direction and passed them. Claire recognised the driver. "Brian! Turn around. That was Livingstone."

"What? Are you sure?" asked Brian, as he hit the brakes.

"One hundred percent."

They were almost at Hermitage Academy so Brian used the small roundabout to head in the opposite direction. Claire made a quick decision. "Blue lights, Brian. Let's let him know we're after him and see what happens."

Brian didn't need to be told twice. He hit the lights and immediately put his foot to the floor, accelerating through the gears. Claire picked up the car radio and called the squad car to explain that they were in pursuit of the suspect and heading towards them. It didn't take Brian long to catch up with Livingstone who was oblivious to the car behind him until he caught sight of the flashing lights in his mirror. Livingstone put his foot on the accelerator and increased the speed of his Ford Escort. He knew he couldn't afford to be caught.

That was the moment when Claire knew that Livingstone had something to hide. However, what happened next was not in the plan. Livingstone flew past the entrance to the Ardardan Estate and headed down the hill towards Cardross where the squad car was waiting for him at the foot of the hill – blue lights flashing. The police car straddled the narrow single-carriageway creating a temporary roadblock. Both police officers, wearing bright yellow high-visibility vests, stood on either side of the vehicle and tried to flag him down, their arms waving furiously to get his attention.

Livingstone panicked and made his first major error of judgement. All his planning, all his hard work was about to unravel as he steered the car at the small gap between the front of the squad car and the farmer's fence on his right.

It didn't take too long for the police officer standing in the gap to realise what was about to happen and quickly jump out of the way.

For a brief moment, Livingstone thought he was high and dry and then disaster struck. The passenger side of his car just caught the bumper of the police vehicle resulting in a sudden change of inertia which turned the vehicle and caused the tail end to skid out of control. Livingstone hit the brakes but it was too late. The car carolled through the fence and dropped down into the field below. The drop was steep and the car rolled over before coming to a sudden stop, upside down, engine running and wheels spinning in the air. The airbags inside the car exploded on impact and protected Livingstone from the worst of the damage, but despite this protection, he cracked his head against the side window of the car and instantly blacked out.

Brian and Claire stopped their car at the newly formed gap in the fence and immediately got out and ran towards the overturned car. Claire climbed down the embankment carefully, followed by Brian, and they cautiously approached the upturned car. Claire went straight to the driver's side and pulled at the door. It was jammed – damaged from the crash. She could see that Livingstone was hanging upside down, being supported by his seat belt.

"Brian!" Claire shouted. "Try the passenger door. I can't get this one opened."

Brian managed to pull the door open and entered the vehicle from the opposite side. He shuffled across the car, prepared himself to hold Livingstone with his stronger right arm and reached up to the seat belt buckle with his weaker left hand. Livingstone dropped down and Brian struggled to hold his weight. His only option was to let

Livingstone slip down onto the inside of the roof of the car which was padded and absorbed some of the impact. Brian turned Livingstone around and dragged him out and away from the vehicle. Claire quickly popped her head inside the vehicle looking for evidence, but could see nothing obvious. "Shit!"

She then tried to open the boot but it was locked. It suddenly occurred to her that the keys were still in the ignition. She leaned back inside the car to reach for them but stopped immediately. There was now a smell of petrol. "Shit!" She scrambled out of the car and ran towards Brian. "Get back!" she screamed.

Brian understood the danger immediately and started to drag Livingstone further away from the vehicle. Claire didn't look back and felt the sudden blast of heat from the explosion as the petrol caught fire and the tank exploded. She fell forward from the force of the blast – hitting the ground hard. All she could think of was the evidence. If it was locked in the boot then it was gone.

Livingstone started to groan as he slowly came around, his eyes blinking at first, adjusting to the light, trying to focus. He stared up at the big policeman in a daze.

"Stay still. An ambulance is on the way," Brian explained.

"Wha…what happened?" asked Livingstone.

"You've been in a crash. Just lie still."

It was not until Claire came up to Livingstone that it all came back to him – the chase, the police car blocking the road, the fence and then... his car! He lifted his head just enough to get a glimpse of the burning car and smiled.

One of the uniformed policemen grabbed a small fire extinguisher from their vehicle and tried to put out the flames, but it made little impact. They would need the fire and rescue service, which was also on its way. The other policeman was up on the road frantically trying to control the traffic, which had started to back up, much to the frustration of the queuing motorists.

Claire sat down on the grass beside Brian and watched the upturned car and any potential evidence inside it burn.

"Are you okay, boss?"

Claire held out her hands. "Yes, a few minor scratches on these, but other than that I'm fine. Thankfully the muddy grass cushioned my fall."

"How are we going to explain this to Carter?" asked Brian.

"Don't worry. It's my fault. If I hadn't instructed you to put on the blue lights, he wouldn't have gone off the road."

"Yeah, but he could have stopped when he saw the car ahead. It was his decision to go off the road."

"Do you think Carter's going to care about that?" said Claire, looking at Brian, seeking confirmation that she was right.

"Probably not," said Brian.

Livingstone attempted to sit up and Brian grabbed him to stop him trying to escape.

"Should I cuff him?" he asked Claire.

"What for? Any evidence there is to link him to the murders is in that bloody car. No, we can't arrest him, but we can escort him safely to the hospital and keep him under observation until we are able to search the car properly."

"Yes, but we could arrest him for reckless driving and refusing to stop."

"Brian, you're a star. What would I do without you? I was so focussed on the murders…" Claire was interrupted by the sound of sirens in the distance. "We'll need to get the traffic moving to allow the emergency vehicles to get here. I'll go up and instruct the uniforms. You stay with him." She pointed to Livingstone. "And, yes, better cuff him in case he gets any more daft ideas."

Brian cautioned Livingstone and then, much to Livingstone's annoyance, he cuffed his hands.

"What are you doing?" asked Livingstone. "You've no right to do this. This is harassment. I'm injured, you know - I thought you said an ambulance is coming."

"Just stay still and you'll be fine, Mr Livingstone. The ambulance will be here as soon as the road clears a bit."

Livingstone looked far from happy but given he couldn't do anything but sit there and wait, he stopped moaning and watched the burning car with some satisfaction. He was more than happy to challenge the alleged driving offences in court.

Meanwhile, Claire had climbed through the gap in the broken fence and back onto the road. She spoke to the young police officer standing there unsure what to do next and instructed him to get the traffic moving, but first he would need to move his vehicle and park it beside the detectives' car.

The car screeched as it started to move - the bent metal of the damaged bumper scraping against the front wheel. Satisfied that one lane of the road was now clear, the police officer jumped out and immediately started to allow the queue of vehicles on the Cardross side to start moving. The paramedic's van was the first emergency vehicle to arrive on the scene and Claire quickly directed the paramedic into the field to treat Livingstone's head wound. It was quickly followed by a fire engine from the nearby Helensburgh Fire Station, then an ambulance, and finally a traffic police vehicle from Dumbarton. They took over the traffic management which allowed the other officers to deal with Livingstone.

Within minutes, the fire service had put out the flames of the burning car and made the vehicle safe. Livingstone, whose head had now been dressed and bound by the paramedic, was breathalysed and was unsurprisingly confirmed as being alcohol-free. He was then taken under police escort to the Royal Alexandria Hospital in Paisley to have his injuries checked by a doctor.

Claire stood with the senior fire service officer and watched as one of the fire officers prised open the twisted boot of the vehicle and revealed the melted remains of what appeared to be a black rubbish bag and a mix of other burned materials. Claire prayed that forensics would be able to find something identifiable in the mess and instructed the fire officer to leave the contents of the boot as he had found them. With her hopes now raised, Claire called Carter to explain what had happened. She requested a SOCO to examine and catalogue the contents of the boot. Carter's initial reaction had been as expected – not good, but the hope of securing evidence to convict Livingstone improved his mood, and he assured Claire that he would get a SOCO there as soon as possible.

Carter was good to his word and the SOCO arrived within fifteen minutes. First things first, the experienced SOCO photographed the scene of the crash, the gap in the fence, the upturned car and then the contents of the boot. Having finished with the camera, he carefully removed the contents of the boot and placed them on a white polythene sheet, took another photograph and then started to open the burned mess of plastic and material. Most of the content was unrecognisable, with the exception of one small item. The SOCO picked up the shiny object using a set of tweezers and placed it onto the plastic sheet and photographed it. He removed a magnifying glass from his case, looked closely and read aloud the tiny engraving on the inside of the ring. "To Grace, with all my love, Barry."

Claire, who had observed all the SOCO's actions, was ecstatic to hear those words. This was the evidence she needed to secure the conviction. She had no doubts that the forensic team would also find evidence of Livingstone's other souvenirs among the burnt waste and possibly even more evidence in Livingstone's mother's house, which would now be searched. She immediately called Carter to give him the good news and could hear the cheers of joy inside the incident room as he relayed this information to the team. When the noise finally subsided, Carter told Claire to remain at the scene until the SOCO had securely bagged all the evidence. Carter would now speak to Milligan and insist on getting a search warrant for the house in Helensburgh. There was still work to be done, but they were confident they had their man. Carter gave the instruction for Livingstone to be arrested on suspicion of murder and brought back to the station for further questioning. They had him!

Chapter 52

The mood in the incident room was still buoyant when Claire and Brian finally made it back to the office. Carter confirmed that the Fiscal had approved the search warrant and that Rambo and Patsy had been sent to Livingstone's mother's house with a couple of SOCOs to check for further evidence.

"Do they know to check the sinks and drains for hair dye?" asked Claire. She had hoped that Carter would have sent her and Brian to search the house but he had other plans for them.

"I'll call Rambo and make sure they do," said Carter. "But I want you to prepare yourself for another interview with Livingstone. You almost got to him last time and this time you have all the evidence you need to get him to confess."

"Yes, boss. Will it be with you or Brian?" she asked.

Carter knew why she was asking, and on another occasion, he might have told her off, but nothing could upset him – not now. "Yes, why not. You two are used to working with each other so sort out your strategy. But understand this, confession or no confession, he will be charged with murder."

~

It was late afternoon by the time that Livingstone was given the all-clear by the hospital and then transported back to the station. He was escorted up to Interview Room 1 by the same two police officers who had attended the scene of the crash. His solicitor, Mr Paul Cairns, arrived shortly after Livingstone and immediately asked to speak to his client in private, which was his right. He was also taken up to the interview room without delay. After a few minutes conferring with his client, he told the officer who was standing guard outside the room that they were ready to speak to the detectives.

Claire and Brian entered the room. Brian turned on the audio recording and Claire stated the names of all present for the record. Carter and Milligan were sitting next door ready to observe the interview.

"Before you begin, Inspector," said Cairns. "Can I request that the handcuffs be removed from my client? He's hardly going to escape from a police station with police officers guarding the door."

"No," Claire replied.

Cairns was clearly taken aback and was lost for words.

"We believe your client to be a dangerous, violent killer. Therefore he will remain handcuffed throughout the duration of this interview," Claire responded.

"Well, in that case, I wish my objection to this barbaric behaviour to be noted on the record."

Livingstone, who had put his cuffed hands up to the desk anticipating that the handcuffs would be removed, was furious, which was exactly what Claire had hoped to achieve. She smiled at him in the hope that this would add to his growing anger.

"Mr Livingstone, what time did you leave your home in Jordanhill this morning?"

"I'm sorry Inspector but I don't see the relevance of that question. I was under the impression that my client has been arrested for the murder of three women," said Cairns.

"That's correct Mr Cairns, but he was also arrested today for dangerous driving and in so doing caused damage to a stationary police vehicle and almost ran over a police officer, so I'll repeat the question. Mr Livingstone, what time did you leave your home in Jordanhill this morning?

Cairns whispered a few words into Livingstone's ear and he nodded in response.

"I left my house at 7.30 a.m. this morning," said Livingstone.

"Did you leave by the front door?"

"No, I left by the back door."

"Really? That's a bit strange. Don't you think?"

"No, I don't," Livingstone responded sharply.

"Correct me if I'm wrong, but you live in a mid-terraced property, Mr Livingstone?"

"Yes," he hissed.

"So, in order to leave by the backdoor, you would need to walk along the back lane and then cut back onto the street through the gap between the end houses."

"That's correct."

"And you don't think that's a bit strange?" Claire asked again.

"No," said Livingstone.

Claire decided to change direction. "You said you left the house at 7.30 a.m. Where were you going so early?"

"I was going to my mother's house. That's not a crime, is it?"

Claire was pleased that he openly admitted that he had gone there. "Why so early, what was the purpose of your trip?"

"I wanted to clean it up a bit before I went into work, Inspector. Is that also a crime?"

"No, that's not a crime, Mr Livingstone, but refusing to stop when directed to do so by a police officer is a crime. Driving recklessly and crashing into a police car is a crime, and killing three innocent women is a crime."

Cairns decided he had heard enough and decided to intervene. "Inspector, my client is willing to admit that he was driving too fast and lost control of his vehicle and accidentally hit the police vehicle. He is fully insured and will happily concede liability for the accident but so far you have not presented one bit of evidence to link my client to the murders of three women."

Claire smiled to herself and again had to admit that Livingstone had come up with another convincing story to explain his behaviour. But he didn't know that Claire had an ace up her sleeve - an ace which she would hold back until the right time. "Patience, Mr Cairns. We will get to the three murders in due course."

"Mr Livingstone, you said you went to your mother's house to clean it up a bit. Where did you clean? The living room?"

"No."

"Hallway?"

"No."

"Kitchen?"

"No."

Bedrooms?"

"No!" he exclaimed.

"Well, that only leaves the bathroom. Did you clean the bathroom, Mr Livingstone?"

"Yes, I cleaned the bloody bathroom, Inspector," moaned Livingstone.

"So, you expect us to believe that you got up early to go to your mother's house to clean the bathroom?"

"Yes, because it's the truth," he hissed.

"Oh, I believe you, Mr Livingstone," said Claire, to his surprise. "I believe you were very keen to clean the sink but you see Mr Livingstone, you might have cleaned the surface of the sink but you didn't clean out the U-bend did you?"

The colour drained from Livingstone's face and Claire knew that she had him worried. The SOCO had indeed found traces of what appeared to be coloured hair dye and coloured hair in the u-bend of the sink. None of it had been tested by the forensic team yet, but Livingstone didn't know that. Claire decided to change direction again and keep Livingstone on edge. "Mr Livingstone, what was in the boot of your car?"

Livingstone knew right away what she was getting at and offered a cautious response. "A spare tyre, a jack, maybe some tools. I can't remember offhand."

"What about the black rubbish bag?"

"Oh, yes, sorry, I forgot about that. I was going to dispose of that after work."

"Do you remember what was in the bag?" she asked.

"Oh, just some rubbish."

"Taken from your mother's house?"

"Yes, I was going to dump it."

"Dump it? Why not put it in the household waste bin at your mother's house?"

"It's mixed waste and the uplift was not due for a couple of weeks."

Another surprisingly quick response from Livingstone. Claire decided it was time to go for the jugular.

"You're a liar Mr Livingstone, aren't you?"

Livingstone and Cairns were stunned by the sudden accusation.

"What?" Livingstone was outraged.

"You're a liar and a killer Mr Livingstone. A brutal, savage killer. Everything you have said today is a lie, isn't it? One huge lie to cover your tracks. I'll tell you what really happened. You killed two innocent women to make the police believe they were after a serial killer and to hide your real target – your ex-wife. And you might have gotten away with it had you not been so arrogant." Claire now had his full attention.

"Did you think we would not make the connection between the dates? You murdered the three women on the birthdays of your ex-wife and daughters and thought that we would not make the connection? Really! You must think we're stupid Mr Livingstone, but I'm afraid you're the only stupid person in this room. A stupid liar."

"Inspector Redding, I really must object to these accusations and insults," said Cairns.

"Be quiet, Mr Cairns. I'm not finished." Both Cairns and Livingstone were livid.

"Who do you think you think you are speaking to… you cheeky little bitch!" Livingston exploded. "Your career is over - you do know that, don't you? This is police harassment. You've had it in for me from the start but you have nothing, so you make up this cock and bull story and are clearly trying to stitch me up."

Claire smiled at Livingstone. She had him where she wanted him. "What's the melting point of gold, Mr Livingstone?" Claire asked.

"What?" said Livingstone, confused by the sudden change in direction.

"Come on, Inspector, I really don't see what possible relevance that question could have to this interview," said Cairns.

She ignored him and continued. "The melting point of gold is 1064 degrees Celsius. Did you know that Mr Livingstone?"

No response. The penny had dropped.

"You see, Mr Livingstone, while most of the contents of the boot of your car were destroyed by the heat of the fire, the temperature was not near hot enough to melt the gold ring that we found there."

Brian took out a clear plastic evidence bag from the folder he was holding and placed it on the desk. Claire lifted the bag and pointed to the small ring which was nested in the bottom right-hand corner. "Do you know who this ring belongs to Mr Livingstone?"

"No, I have never seen it before."

"No, but it was found in the boot of your car. It belongs to Grace Anderson, the first murder victim. It was her wedding band. How did it get there, Mr Livingstone?"

Livingstone finally snapped. "You did it. You must have planted it there when I was unconscious." He turned towards Cairns. "Don't you see, this confirms what I have said all along – she's out to get me and now she's even planting evidence! She'll stop at nothing to get me."

Cairns turned to Claire. "Well, Inspector?"

Claire nodded to Brian who took out a photograph from the table and placed it in front of Livingstone. "These are the photographs taken from the body of Grace Anderson by a Scenes of Crime Officer in Coatbridge, just a few hours after the discovery of her body. Do you see the white skin above the engagement ring? According to her husband, Grace Anderson always wore her wedding band; she never took it off, which means her killer must have removed it. So, my question to you, Mr Livingstone, is this: if I planted the ring, as you have just suggested, how did I get it to plant it? I wasn't involved in the initial investigation in Coatbridge. I've had no contact with Grace

Anderson's body. The police there did not even know that the ring was missing. So how could I possibly get hold of the ring to plant it in the boot of your car?"

There was silence. Claire could tell from Cairn's face that there was no way back for his client.

"Well, Mr Livingstone? Can you explain how the ring belonging to Grace Anderson found its way into your car? Oh, and by the way, our forensic team will examine the other burnt contents of your boot and I'm guessing we will also find evidence of a facemask and a broken heel of a shoe. Well, Mr Livingstone, can you explain it?"

"No comment!" Livingstone replied through gritted teeth.

"Thought so. Iain Livingstone, you are charged with the murder of Grace Anderson, Jackie Ross and Sheila Maxwell. Do you have anything further to say in your defence?"

"You fucking bitch!" he shouted from across the table.

"I beg your pardon," said Claire, hoping that he would repeat what he just said. The audio was still recording.

Cairns put his hand on Livingstone's arm to calm him down.

"Don't touch me, you useless wanker!" Livingstone spat out at Cairns, who immediately withdrew his arm.

"You smart-arsed little bitch. Oh, you think you're so clever, don't you? Just you wait and see, I'll get you."

Claire smiled calmly at Livingstone. Her strategy had worked. She knew if she presented the ring first, he would say nothing and the remainder of the interview would be pointless as he would revert to the classic "no comment". But, by delaying and getting him talking about areas he was confident he could explain, she had opened the door to reveal his true nature: his fierce, vicious, violent temper, which he had hidden so well in previous interviews. "You know Mr Livingstone, I might be very smart but there's one thing I still haven't worked out, so perhaps you could enlighten me. Why did you wait eight years before deciding to take your revenge on Sheila? I know that your mother died but I still don't …"

"Well, you wouldn't, would you, detective? You're just another one of them. A pathetic little woman who has been given a taste of power and you just love it, don't you? Look at you, with your pretty little face and your smug, patronising little smile. No, you wouldn't understand, you're not capable of understanding, none of you are."

"Well then, help me out here. Explain it to me."

Tears started to form in Livingstone's eyes as he replayed the painful memory of his mother's funeral. "It wasn't enough that she humiliated me -

took my house, took my girls. No, she had the fucking audacity to turn up at my mother's funeral and rub it in my face. The bitch! The fucking twisted little bitch. My mother was never the same after the divorce. She was heartbroken. She loved those girls but they stopped visiting her - thanks to Sheila. So, you see Inspector, Sheila wasn't innocent, none of them were innocent. They all got what they fucking deserved!"

Claire stood up, content that she had all she needed. "You're right, Mr Livingstone. I don't understand. Interview terminated at 5.45 p.m."

Chapter 53

Claire woke before her alarm went off. She felt like she had barely slept a wink, such was the excitement of the previous day but instead of feeling tired and lethargic, she felt the opposite - she felt alive, completely and utterly alive. She decided to go for a run before breakfast and quickly got dressed and went downstairs. Peter grunted something unintelligible and then went back to sleep.

Claire picked up her mobile phone and turned it on - she would listen to her favourite playlist on Spotify while running. As she flicked through the menu, a message flashed on her screen.

You have a voicemail. Call 121 to listen to your message. Message received at 11.13 p.m. Claire clicked on the phone icon and could see DSup Mulholland had called. She dialled 121 to listen to the message and then pressed 1 to hear new messages. *Must be important if he called at that time of night.*

The message played: 'Hi Claire, sorry to disturb you so late, but thought you might want to know the latest news in connection with Petrie. You'll remember that we thought that Baxter was responsible for his death. Well, we carried out a raid on one of Baxter's offices tonight, which allowed our tech boys to carry out a search of his accounts. We tried searching on Petrie's name, not really expecting to find anything but came across a record of an international bank transfer from a company called P&SMAC Holdings, that's Papa, Ampersand, Sierra, Mike, Alpha, Charlie. We asked Interpol to take a look and it appears that the money, a sum of £100,000, was transferred from a Swiss Bank Account in Zurich, just days before Petrie's murder. If I were a gambling man, I would bet that Baxter was paid by an unnamed third party to kill Petrie, or at least that's the theory that we're now working on. Unfortunately, that's where the trail ends. The Swiss are really tight on releasing bank account information to anyone, including the Police. Anyway, the reason why I'm calling was just to check if the name P&SMAC Holdings meant anything to you. Did it appear anywhere in the McGrath investigation? Give me a call if you can think of anything. Thanks.'

Claire ended the voicemail call. She sat on the foot of the stairs thinking about the message and concluded that P&SMAC Holdings meant nothing to her. She was sure it hadn't come up during McGrath's investigation but there was something else niggling her about it which she couldn't quite put her finger on. After a minute of raking through the annals of her memory, she gave up trying. She set up her playlist, pressed her earphones gently into each ear and left the house by the front door. She headed towards the cycle path to start her morning run and stopped at the bridge over the burn to stretch her leg muscles and then took off towards Bowling.

She was completely unaware that he was following her and he was pleased to see that she was wearing her earphones - that would make it easier for him to complete his task. He had it all worked out, it was just a matter of timing.

Chapter 54

Dressed in his running gear and jogging at the same pace as Claire, the assassin followed her along the cycle path. They had now reached the stretch that ran parallel with the A82 and were heading towards Bowling, where the runners would need to cross the A814 to connect to the other side of the cycle path. They were surrounded by trees full of birds singing their morning songs, but as they got closer to the Bowling roundabout, the sound of cars on the A82 could be heard. *It was all a matter of timing.* As he reached the small hill, he started to speed up, closing in on Claire, preparing to strike.

Claire was enjoying the run but all she could think about was P&SMAC and why it meant something to her. It repeated over and over again in her head. *P&SMAC, P&SMAC, P&SMAC.* And then, out of the blue, it struck her like a lightning bolt. *Oh my God, Peter and Sally Macdonald!* She passed through the gate at the top of the hill and stopped dead in her tracks, overcome by the significance of her discovery.

The assassin, who had been accelerating and had almost caught her, did not anticipate that she would stop suddenly and his momentum took him right into her. He had no option other than to push as hard as he could, projecting her into the oncoming traffic on the road ahead but not as he had planned. Not under control - stopping himself, before the exit, safe and out of sight of any motorists. No, he stumbled into her and could not stop himself, stumbling, falling onto the road. *Timing was everything.* Claire tumbled onto the road into a gap in the traffic on the nearside carriageway but was hit by a car on the other side of the road. She rolled over the bonnet of a small Volkswagen Polo, cracked her head off the windscreen and fell onto the ground, stunned, unconscious, motionless, but not dead. Fortunately for Claire, the Polo had been braking to take the turn and the impact on her body was not as severe as it could have been.

The assassin was less fortunate. He stumbled forward into the path of a lorry on the nearside carriageway, was hit by the front of the large vehicle and bounced forward onto the road. The shocked lorry driver hit his brakes as hard and as fast as he could but there was no way he could miss the fallen runner. The sound of crushing bones and screams of pain could be heard as the assassin's neck and head were crushed under the weight of the three-tonne vehicle, resulting in his instant death. The drivers of both vehicles involved in the accident got out and ran to the aid of the two runners. The lorry driver emptied the contents of his stomach onto the side of the road, as the sight of the splattered blood and grey matter was too much for him to handle. The female driver of the Polo knelt down beside Claire. A trained first aider, she checked Claire's pulse, which was weak, and then confirmed that she was still breathing by putting her ear to Claire's lips. The relief she felt was almost euphoric. She stood up and shouted over to the lorry driver to call an ambulance, which he did after wiping the puke from his mouth.

The police were first to arrive on the scene and it didn't take long for one of the officers to recognise that one of the injured runners was their DI. The news spread quickly and no one was more shocked than Peter to find out that once again, Claire was in hospital – this time, as the result of an accident and not in the line of duty.

Peter called Claire's mum and dad and agreed to meet them at the Royal Alexandria Hospital in Paisley where Claire had been admitted and was being treated for various injuries, including concussion. Brian also got the message, but he was with Agnes, who was being prepared for her operation and therefore he could not leave her side.

Chapter 55

Peter, Claire's mum and dad and DCI Carter were waiting impatiently in the small hospital waiting room which was located just outside the surgical ward where Claire had been admitted. After a lengthy wait, Dr Narayan Sharma, wearing blue surgical gowns and a mask, entered the waiting room.

Peter was the first to react and was on his feet as soon as the door opened. "How is she, doctor, is she okay? I mean, will she be okay?"

"Are you her husband?" Dr Sharma asked.

"Yes, Peter Macdonald," he responded.

Dr Sharma looked around the room. "Are you all relatives?"

"This is Claire's mum and dad," he said, pointing to the couple who were now on their feet desperate to hear news of their daughter. "And this is DCI Carter, Claire's boss."

Carter stood in response to his name. "I'll be outside," he offered, reading the situation. It was clear that the doctor was about to deliver some bad news to the family.

Peter turned to Carter. "Thanks. I'll let you know the situation after the doctor has finished. Carter nodded in response and left the room.

"Please, everyone, take a seat," suggested Dr Sharma, who waited until all three had sat down before continuing. "First of all, Claire's condition is stable, she has suffered some internal injuries which we have dealt with. She is badly concussed and appears to have experienced some short-term memory loss, which is to be expected following such a trauma." He paused, composed himself and looked directly at Peter. "I'm afraid that she's lost the baby. I really am very sorry. We managed to stop the internal bleeding, but it was too late to save the baby. I'm sorry."

Peter could not speak. He collapsed into a chair as the shocking reality of the situation sank in and then the tears came. His perfect world had been shattered, and the pain that he felt far outweighed anything that he had experienced as a child.

John Redding was the first to gain enough composure to speak. "Doctor, will Claire be able to have other children?

Peter had not even considered this possibility and stood up to receive the response.

"I'm afraid, we had to carry out an emergency hysterectomy to stop the bleeding."

Peter slumped back down into the chair. He didn't need to be told what that meant. Any chance of him and Claire having a family of their own had gone as a result of one terrible accident. Yes, he was relieved that Claire had survived the accident and they would carry on regardless but nothing would ever be the same. John Redding hugged his wife, Margaret, who was now in tears on hearing the terrible news.

"Does Claire know yet?" Peter asked.

"No, she's still recovering from the operation. I, eh, thought it might be better for Claire to hear it from you… once the effects of the anaesthetic have worn off," explained Dr Sharma.

Peter nodded. "Yes, I guess it should be me." He had no idea how he was going to be strong enough to share the news with Claire without crumbling into a complete wreck, but he had to be strong. Now, more than ever, he had to be the strong one.

Chapter 56

"Hello Jim, it's Brian, any news about Claire?" Brian was sitting in a waiting room in the Queen Elizabeth University Hospital in Glasgow, where Agnes was undergoing her surgery.

"Hi, Sarge. Sorry, no, nothing from the hospital yet. DCI Carter is there and has promised to let us know as soon as he hears anything. It sounds pretty bad though - she was still unconscious when the ambulance arrived."

"Christ. That's not good. What about the other guy?"

"He'd no chance. Apparently, he was run over by a lorry. Crushed his skull. The SOC team are still on site, picking up the pieces. It's a real mess, not to mention the traffic chaos with the roads being closed."

"Have you managed to identify him yet?

"No, but the SOCO has sent in an e-copy of his fingerprints to check on the system. There's no chance that we'll get facial or dental recognition."

"It was that bad, then?" asked Brian.

"So, I hear. Sounds like the boss was lucky by all accounts?"

"Yes, well, let me know if you hear anything, Jim."

"Will do Sarge. You can count on it. Eh… how's Agnes doing?"

"Still in surgery. Shouldn't be too long now."

"Well, I hope she's okay and the operation's a success."

"Thanks, Jim, me too. Take care." Brian ended the call and looked at his watch. He hated waiting.

~

Over an hour after being told the news about losing the baby, Peter was finally allowed in the room to see Claire. She was still pretty groggy from the anaesthetic but was awake.

Peter approached the bed and gently held Claire's hand in his. "Hello, love, how are you feeling?"

Claire turned her head slowly to look at Peter. "What happened?"

"You've been in an accident, Claire. Don't you remember?"

She shook her head slowly.

"Well, you were hit by a car when crossing the road at Bowling. The surgeon says you're going to be fine but you've lost …" Tears began to stream from his eyes.

"The baby!" Claire cried out, tears now forming in her eyes.

Peter couldn't speak and just nodded in confirmation. He sat there feeling hopeless. He was unable to say anything that might console Claire and unable to console himself, such was the depth of his grief. And so, he just sat there in silence holding her hand in his hand. He didn't have the heart to tell her about the hysterectomy. That could wait.

Claire was in shock and was struggling to understand what had happened to her. Was this real or just a bad dream? She tried desperately to remember what had happened. She was running, listening to music … and then what. *"The road!"* she exclaimed. And then it started to come back to her gradually: images of the road, a car, the screeching of brakes, the pain, her body tumbling… and then nothing. She touched the bandage on her head. She had hit the windscreen. And then … *I was pushed.* "Peter," she whispered. "Another runner?"

Peter managed to compose himself before responding. "Do you remember now? That's good. That's a good sign. The doctor said …"

Claire gripped his hand to stop him from speaking. "The other runner, is he here?"

"No, he wasn't as fortunate as you. He didn't make it."

"He's dead?"

"Yes, crushed by a lorry, poor sod."

"He pushed me," said Claire.

"What? What do you mean, he pushed you? What, deliberately?"

Claire nodded. Peter's grief suddenly turned to anger. It was bad enough when he thought it was an accident, but this… this was something else altogether. "Did you recognise him?"

Claire shook her head. She hadn't seen his face; he had pushed her from behind when she had stopped… and then she remembered why she had stopped running. *P&SMAC!*

Peter didn't notice the change in Claire's demeanour. He was too busy pacing up and down the room to notice anything. He decided he had to tell Carter, he had to find out who this man was. This man, who had killed his child and had killed his hopes of having a family. "Claire, your mum and dad are outside waiting to see you. I'll go and get them."

Before she could stop him, he was gone. He quickly explained to the Reddings that Claire knew that she had lost the baby but not the rest; that would be too much for Claire to cope with in her current fragile state. They nodded in full understanding and entered the room, leaving Peter with Carter.

"We need to talk," said Peter.

Chapter 57

Carter called Police HQ in Dumbarton to prioritise the identity check on the dead runner. Now that he was suspected of the attempted murder of a police officer, it was even more critical to find out who he was and, perhaps more importantly, why he wanted to kill Claire.

The news of this latest revelation sent shock waves around the police station and within minutes, the search for the identity of the mystery runner was intensified. Within an hour, a fingerprint match was found and the man was identified as Victor Cortez, a known assassin and number five on Interpol's list of wanted criminals. He had operated all over Europe, selling his deadly skills to those wealthy enough to pay and, like his rich clients, Mr Cortez kept his cash in Switzerland.

DCI Morrison had been alerted to the news and took over the investigation; she would not rest until they found who had paid the assassin. Unsurprisingly, Interpol had confirmed that Cortez had kept his money in Switzerland and were just as keen as Police Scotland to get their hands on his account details. On this occasion, however, the Swiss banks would be more cooperative because the account holder was dead and they had no client to protect. Unlike Interpol, Police Scotland were only interested in one transaction: the last one! A few hours later, the information requested was sent by email to Police HQ, in Dumbarton.

As soon as DCI Mitchell received the paperwork, she called Carter to give him the news. The payment had been received from a Scottish bank account. A bank account, held by a Scottish company registered as East End Entities. It didn't take long for the police to establish that the company was owned by Robert Petrie, deceased.

Carter was told the news and immediately went looking for Peter. He found him in the room sitting alone with Claire - her mum and dad had gone home and had promised to return later. Carter popped his head around the door. "Peter, can I have a word?"

"Sure." He kissed Claire on the cheek and then headed for the door.

"What's up?"

"We've identified the man who pushed Claire."

"That was quick. Who is he?"

"His name is Victor Cortez. He's an assassin."

"What? Why would anyone want ..." Peter's heart sank with the sudden realisation of the truth.

"Did Claire tell you about a drug dealer called Petrie?"

Peter's heart sank. "Yes, but he's dead. He was killed in prison a few days ago."

"Yes, but it appears that he managed to order the hit before he died."

"But I don't understand. He was in prison. How could he do that from there?"

"That's what DCI Mitchell is going to find out, and believe me, she won't stop until we get everyone involved. He's clearly had someone working for him on the outside and we'll get them. I'm sorry Peter. I need to get back to the station but if there's anything we can do, just let me know."

"Sure, and thanks for being here. It's appreciated."

Carter turned and headed down the long corridor towards the exit. Peter turned back into the private room where Claire was waiting patiently to find out what was going on. It was time to tell her about the hysterectomy and time to tell her about Petrie.

The end

Other books by Andrew Hawthorne

There's no such thing as a perfect crime (DI Redding Series, Book 1)

The Keeper (DI Redding Series, Book 2)

A Mug's Game (DI Redding Series, Book 3)

For Children

Who put that spaceship on my school?!

Printed in Great Britain
by Amazon